From the Ashes

Patricia H. Rushford

Books by Patricia Rushford

Young Adult Fiction

JENNIE MCGRADY MYSTERIES

1. *Too Many Secrets*
2. *Silent Witness*
3. *Pursued*
4. *Deceived*
5. *Without a Trace*
6. *Dying to Win*
7. *Betrayed*
8. *In Too Deep*
9. *Over the Edge*
10. *From the Ashes*

Adult Fiction

Morningsong

HELEN BRADLEY MYSTERIES

1. *Now I Lay Me Down to Sleep*
2. *Red Sky in Mourning*

9708

From the Ashes

Patricia H. Rushford

BETHANY HOUSE PUBLISHERS
MINNEAPOLIS, MINNESOTA 55438

From the Ashes
Copyright © 1997
Patricia Rushford

Cover illustration by Sergio Giovine

Published by Bethany House Publishers
A Ministry of Bethany Fellowship, Inc.
11300 Hampshire Avenue South
Minneapolis, Minnesota 55438

Printed in the United States of America.

Library of Congress Cataloging-in-Publication Data

Rushford, Patricia H.
From the ashes / by Patricia H. Rushford.
p. cm. — (Jennie McGrady mystery ; #10)
Summary: Jennie searches for the person responsible for burning down the buildings that comprised her beloved church and school.
ISBN 1-55661-563-9 (pbk.)
[1. Arson—Fiction. 2. Christian life—Fiction. 3. Mystery and detective stories.] I. Title. II. Series: Rushford, Patricia H. Jennie McGrady mystery series ; 10.
PZ7.R8962Fr 1997
[Fic]—dc21 97-21124
CIP
AC

For Corisa Lester and Jennifer Anderson
and for friendships that last forever.

A special thanks to Evelyn Larkin and Birdie Etchison
as well as the Clark County Medical Examiner's office,
and Vancouver police and fire fighters—
especially to Don Phillips and Don McCoy
for lending a degree of authenticity to *From the Ashes*.

PATRICIA RUSHFORD is an award-winning writer, speaker, and teacher who has published numerous articles and over twenty-five books, including *What Kids Need Most in a Mom, The Jack and Jill Syndrome: Healing for Broken Children*, and *Have You Hugged Your Teenager Today?* She is a registered nurse and has a master's degree in counseling from Western Evangelical Seminary. She and her husband, Ron, live in Washington State and have two grown children, six grandchildren, and lots of nephews and nieces.

Pat has been reading mysteries for as long as she can remember and is delighted to be writing a series of her own. She is a member of Mystery Writers of America, Sisters in Crime, and several other writing organizations. She is also the co-director of Writer's Weekend at the Beach.

1

"Jennie, pull over. Hurry!" Lisa urged. "We have to let them get by."

"I'm trying." Jennie McGrady nosed her red Mustang into the right lane of traffic. Sirens howled and horns tooted through the hot and hazy September afternoon. Jennie's thoughts quickly turned from cooling off in their friends' swimming pool in Lake Oswego to merging with the dozens of other vehicles that clogged the four-lane boulevard.

A hard knot formed in the pit of her stomach as four red fire trucks and two ambulances whizzed by. The heavy traffic impeded their progress, and Jennie hoped they'd make it through in time to wherever they had to go.

"Oh wow. I wonder if that's where they're going. Looks like a huge fire." Lisa, Jennie's cousin and best friend, rolled down the window and leaned out to get a better view.

Jennie scanned the blue sky, her gaze coming to rest on billowing black clouds barely visible over the tree-covered hillside. She eased her car back into traffic, staying in the outside lane in case other emergency units needed by. They had gone only a short distance when sirens split the air again. Police cars this time.

"Oh no." Lisa covered her mouth, and panic filled her green eyes. "What if it's . . . no, I can't say it."

She didn't have to. The billowing fireball seemed to be

emerging from the woods near their church and school. "Trinity's not the only building over there," Jennie reminded her. "The fire looks close, but it could be farther away."

"I . . . I know. Let's go by the church to make sure."

Jennie nodded, turning onto Brentwood Road. The two-lane road meandered up the hill, past elegant homes snuggled between stately evergreens. She could smell the smoke that settled over them like a menacing fog. Neither of them spoke as they watched the fire now only a short distance in front of them. Just ahead, two police cars blocked the road, their lights flashing. Two uniformed officers were setting out flares and barricades. Several cars were parked on the street, and a crowd had already gathered.

"It is Trinity! I knew it." Lisa gripped the door handle.

"At least wait until I stop." Jennie jammed on the brakes, pulled over to the side of the road, and jumped out, tearing ahead of her cousin. The searing fire had bumped the heat up from 90 degrees to at least 110. Still she ran toward the flames, drawn by the choking fear that someone she knew might be hurt.

"Hey, you can't go in there!" one of the officers yelled.

Jennie dodged her and kept running.

"No!" Lisa screamed. "Let me go!"

Jennie glanced back. The other officer had Lisa pinned against him, her arms and legs flailing as she tried to escape. "Let me go!"

Jennie slowed. *What are you doing, McGrady? You just went through a police barricade.*

The officer chasing her caught Jennie by the arm and spun her around. "I told you to stop. You can't go in there."

"It's our school—and church. . . ." Jennie stammered. "I need to help."

The officer's anger subsided. "I'm sorry, but there's nothing you can do. We've got orders not to let anyone in there. It's too dangerous. You need to vacate the area."

Jennie looked at the officer for the first time, letting her gaze drift over the woman's frosted hair, into her dark brown eyes, and down to her badge and a name pin that read *B. Saunders*. Her bulletproof vest made her slender figure thicker, more masculine looking.

"Do . . . do you know how bad it is?" Jenny asked. "Or if anyone was hurt?"

Saunders shook her head. "I haven't heard. Just got orders to keep people out."

"Jennie!" Lisa cried. "Make him let go of me." Her face nearly matched the color of her red curls. Two more police vehicles had arrived.

Jennie frowned at the handcuffs he pulled out. "You're not going to arrest her, are you?"

"Come on, Calahan. Cut her some slack. It's their school," Saunders explained. "And church."

"That may be," Calahan growled, "but we've got our orders."

One of the new officers put a bullhorn to his mouth. "Listen up. We have orders to evacuate the area. Please move back."

An unmarked police car pulled in behind Jennie's Mustang. A familiar dark-haired detective emerged.

"Dad!" Jennie barreled toward him, stopping just short of flinging herself into his arms.

"What are you doing out here?" He didn't seem very happy to see her.

"Lisa and I were headed over to the Beaumonts' to swim. We saw the smoke and thought it might be . . ." A lump clogged her throat. She managed to say, "Dad, it's Trinity."

His arm went around her shoulders as he guided her back up to where Lisa was still being detained. "I know. I heard the call on my way home." Jason McGrady was a homicide detective for the Portland Police.

"Can't we do something?" Jennie asked.

"That's what I'm here to find out."

"Uncle Jason, I'm so glad to see you." Lisa brushed a hand across her eyes. "Make them let me go."

"What's going on?" Jason McGrady showed the officers his badge and introduced himself.

"You know these kids?" Calahan asked.

"Yes, this is my daughter, and the one you're holding is my niece."

"Better get them out of here. We've got a four-alarm fire up there. Doesn't look good."

"Come on, girls."

"Can't we stay here with you?" Jennie pleaded. "We won't get in the way."

"No. Not a good idea," Dad said. "I'll try to get some details and let you know as soon as I can."

Heading back to the car, Lisa mumbled something about Officer Calahan's bad manners. "Uncle Jason should have punched him out."

"Let it go, Lisa." Jennie glanced behind her at the still flashing lights. "They were only doing their jobs. We're lucky they didn't book us—especially you. It's against the law to hit a police officer. The poor guy's legs are going to be black-and-blue."

Lisa sniffed, wiping away the last traces of tears with the back of her hand. "I suppose you're right. I just feel so—so angry. I wanted to see for myself. I wanted to do something."

"Yeah. Me too. But like Dad said, we'll be more help if we let the fire department take care of things. That's the only—"

An explosion rocked the ground. Jennie staggered back.

"Get down!" Dad shouted.

Jennie dove to the asphalt, taking Lisa with her.

Seconds later the hillside sat in stony silence. Debris rained down on them. Jennie felt numb and disoriented. Her elbow burned where she'd scraped it on the rocks. The pungent smell of smoke nearly overpowered the tar from the road. Sharp pebbles bit into her bare legs and the side of her cheek.

Jennie rolled onto her back, sat up, and brushed herself off, staring at the blood oozing out a small cut on the back of her hand.

"This can't be happening." Lisa picked a patch of tar from her knee.

As if to argue the point, a piece of charred paper floated down, landing in front of them. Jennie picked it up. If she'd needed proof, there it was in black and white. Trinity's letterhead with half the page burned. The only words still legible was their mission statement: *A community of caring people serving you.* An embossed cross making up the "T" in Trinity was all that remained of the heading. Jennie swallowed hard, biting into her lower lip to keep it from trembling.

2

Dad and the other officers checked Jennie and Lisa for injuries. Dad dug a bandage out of the first-aid kit in his trunk and carefully placed it on Jennie's hand. "We need to get you two out of here. Can you drive, Jennie?"

Jennie nodded. When he opened the car door for her, she slid in. As if on automatic pilot, Jennie pulled the seat belt around her and buckled it. The scene was like something you might see in a war movie. Not something that happened in an elite neighborhood near Portland, Oregon.

Officer Saunders helped Lisa in on the passenger side, then reached across to buckle her in.

"Are you sure you can make it out of here all right?" Dad clasped Jennie's shoulder.

Jennie assured him she was fine. Fumbling with the keys, she managed to start the car, turn it around, and drive back down the hill.

"I don't know how you can be so calm." Lisa glanced at Jennie, her green eyes still registering shock.

Jennie blinked back a new rush of tears. *Calm?* She was anything but. She'd learned in her life-saving classes through the Red Cross that you can't panic. You do what you have to do, then when it's all over, you can fall apart. "Somebody has to stay calm. Since I'm driving it better be me."

Lisa leaned back against the seat and stared at her watch.

"I wonder if it's on television yet."

"Probably." Jennie's gaze lingered for a moment on her cousin. Lisa's copper curls hung in disarray as damp tendrils clung to her cheeks. Black smudges smeared her freckled face and her fluorescent lime T-shirt. She looked as bad as Jennie felt.

Jennie's hands were beginning to shake. *Hold on, McGrady. Just a little farther.* Jennie turned right on Lakeview Drive, then made a left into the Beaumonts' driveway. The castle-like home sat on a hill, surrounded by a moat of luxurious green grass. At one time the Beaumont mansion had seemed foreboding and threatening. Now Jennie felt almost as comfortable there as in her own home.

"I wonder where Rafael and his dad are?" Lisa scanned the grounds, looking for the gardeners. She'd developed a crush on Rafael Hernandez, and they'd gone out a couple of times. Jennie had hoped to see them as well. Mr. Hernandez's brother, Philippe, and his son Carlos had only recently come to the U.S. on a work release. Philippe was the janitor at Trinity.

"I hope Philippe and Carlos are okay," Jennie voiced her thoughts. "They would have been there."

"Oh, Jennie, please don't say anything. I don't even want to think about who might be there."

Glancing back in the direction of the church, they could see the thick columns of smoke still pouring out. What had once been a beautiful complex with a blue-tiled roof was now an inferno. Names and faces of people she knew and cared about moved through Jennie's mind. She blocked them out. Like Lisa, she didn't want to think about the dozens of people who could have been inside. Jennie jerked her gaze back to the house, bringing the Mustang to a stop in the turnaround.

Allison and B.J. clamored down the steps, nearly tripping each other in the process. "Where have you been?"

"Did you get caught in the traffic?"

"Did you hear about the fire? What happened to you?"

"Hurry up—they're talking about it on the news."

Jennie didn't know who had asked what and let Lisa answer their questions. They hurried inside and up to Allison's room on the second floor, where Jennie plopped on the bed and sat cross-legged. "Shhh. They're putting someone in an ambulance."

"There must be a lot of injuries." B.J. scrambled onto the bed beside Jennie and punched the control to turn up the volume.

"Firefighters are still battling the blaze near Lake Oswego today. Residents reported the fire at four this afternoon. By the time firefighters arrived the blaze had consumed much of the facility. And just a few minutes ago we received word of an explosion. Authorities have evacuated the area. We have Brenda Ellis at the scene. Brenda, what can you tell us?"

The cameras shifted from the newsroom to a reporter standing near police cars. "It's utter chaos out here, Mike. As you can see, the fire is still burning out of control. I'm standing in front of the police barricade. No one is allowed in other than emergency vehicles. They are especially wary now because of the explosion."

"Any word on what caused that, Brenda?"

"Just speculation at this point, but one firefighter told me it may have been the oil furnace. I have the pastor of the church, Reverend Dave Wilson, here with me. Reverend, can you tell us what happened?"

The camera zoomed in on Pastor Dave. He brought a fist to his mouth and coughed. His face was smudged with black smoke. "We were having a board meeting this afternoon when the fire broke out. We're guessing it started in the basement—maybe the furnace. It all happened so fast we barely had time to escape."

Allison grabbed B.J.'s arm. "Oh, I just remembered. Daddy was at that meeting."

"I know." B.J. pulled her arm away. "Just listen."

"I understand there were at least a dozen people inside. Did everyone make it out all right?" Brenda asked.

"As far as I know. I'm not sure who all was in the building. It's been so chaotic. Michael—our youth director—went back in to check. I don't know if he made it out before the explosion."

Jennie's heart dropped to the pit of her stomach. "What about Michael? What happened to Michael?"

Michael Rhodes had come to Trinity a little over a year ago and had taken over the position of youth director that summer. He had been engaged to Jennie's mother and they'd almost married. At the time, Jennie's father was missing and presumed dead. Then Dad came home and changed everything. Jennie was thrilled to have her family back together but felt sad for Michael. She'd hated him at first, but she'd grown to love and admire him, as had all the kids at Trinity. He really cared about helping them.

Please, God, Jennie offered up a silent prayer. *Let Michael be okay.*

"Let's hope he did. We have no word yet on how many people have been injured." The reporter glanced at a note pad, then asked, "The complex not only houses a church but a school as well, isn't that right?"

"Yes, the church is the central-most part. It separates the grade school, K through eight, and the high school." Pastor Dave turned away and coughed against the back of his hand.

"Since this is a school day, do you know if there were any students or teachers left in the building?"

He shook his head. "Not for certain." His voice broke. "I'm sorry. This is difficult. It's almost too much to comprehend."

Brenda turned back to the camera. "As Pastor Wilson said, it is almost incomprehensible. No one here can be certain of anything, except that one of the largest and most diverse churches in the area is under siege. The loss to students and to church members as well as to the community will be devastating."

The camera pulled back, showing the newsroom and the live action scene.

"Brenda, is there any word yet on how the fire started?" the anchorman asked.

"No. It's too soon to tell, but because of the way the fire spread so rapidly, they suspect arson."

"Thanks, Brenda." He turned away from the monitor and looked into the camera. "This is the third church fire in the Portland area. Last June, arsonists destroyed the First Baptist Church in the Rosewood district. Two months before that, a fire gutted St. Mary's in Beaverton. No arrests have been made, and both cases are still under investigation. Authorities are not saying for certain, but there is speculation the three fires may be related."

Jennie fell back against the pillow. *Arson*. The ugly word seeped into her mind like the thick black smoke that was once again filling the television screen.

"Who'd want to burn down Trinity?" Allison pushed the mute button when the station went to a commercial break. Tears pooled in her eyes as she spoke.

"I can't believe it." Lisa paced to the window. "It's too awful."

Jennie couldn't believe it either but didn't say so. Allison and Lisa found it hard to envision anyone doing anything that bad. They didn't want to think people had a dark and evil side. Jennie had seen it once too often. B.J. had too. Which is why her response didn't surprise Jennie one bit.

"I'll bet it was a hate crime. Somebody who didn't like what Trinity was doing."

"What could anybody object to?" Lisa swung back around and leaned against the windowsill.

"There have been a lot of changes at Trinity since Michael came on staff, and even more with Pastor Cole." B.J. stared at the television screen as she spoke.

"That's dumb. Having a black pastor on staff is a good thing, isn't it?" Allison picked up a ruffled pink pillow and hugged it. "I like Pastor Cole. She's so . . . colorful."

"Of course it's good," B.J. answered, glancing at her sister, then back at the screen where another stupid commercial with talking pets advertised dog food. "So is the AIDS program and offering our sanctuary to minorities for their church services. But not everybody agrees. There are even people in our church who don't like what's going on. Dad said a couple of the board members were really miffed about some of the changes."

"Sure, but enough to burn down their own church?" Allison flipped the pillow aside and slumped deeper into her chair.

"Well," Lisa said, "if we're going to start listing suspects, we should add that neo-Nazi creep, Jared."

"You mean the guy who came to our youth group Saturday night?" Allison sniffed, then retrieved a box of tissues from her dresser.

"Yeah. Rafael says he's bad news. Jared hates everyone who isn't white."

With her eyes still closed, Jennie pictured Jared Reinhardt. Tall, thin, average-looking, with a pointy chin and chiseled features. What little hair he had was blond. He'd shaved it all off and it was just beginning to grow back.

Michael had been counseling Jared, helping him break free of a neo-Nazi group he'd hooked up with—at least that's what Jared had told her. Jennie felt sorry for him and had accepted an invitation to go with him for ice cream after the youth meeting. That had been two days ago. Though she wasn't interested in him as a boyfriend, he'd touched a cord in her. He seemed lost and scared—almost desperate. Of course, some of the kids at the meeting hadn't helped—Lisa included. They'd been uncharacteristically rude. Now listening to Lisa, Jennie understood why.

"Good call, Lisa." B.J. shifted and nudged Jennie. "What do you think, McGrady?"

Jennie opened her eyes and looked from one to the other. She wasn't ready to defend Jared—at least not yet. But she wasn't ready to suspect him of arson either. "Why ask me?"

B.J. shrugged. "Thought you might have an opinion."

"I think it's too soon to speculate. You don't have any facts to back up your argument. We should wait for the fire department to tell us whether or not it's arson. Then we can talk about who might have done it."

"Jennie's right," Allison said. "Let's wait until we have all the facts before—"

"Hey." B.J. pointed to the television set and pressed the mute button. "They're talking about the fire again."

Cameras focused in on an ambulance. Paramedics were putting someone inside.

"Can you see who it is?" Lisa asked.

None of them could. The ambulance drove off and the reporter came back into view.

"Ambulance crews have taken five people to the hospital so far, but we don't yet know the extent of their injuries. Authorities are withholding names until relatives can be reached."

They pulled back, showing a wide-angle view, then an aerial shot. "The fire continues to burn, though firefighters say they should soon have the upper hand. And we do have some good news. Fire chief Ron Hughes tells me all of the people believed to have been in the building are now out. Back to you, Mike."

"Good news, indeed." In the next breath he went on to report about some senator who was under investigation for fraud.

Jennie let out the breath she'd been holding. Michael had

escaped and so had Philippe and Carlos. She just hoped no one had gone in undetected—that the students and teachers and volunteers were all safe.

The phone rang somewhere downstairs. "Allison, B.J.!" Mrs. Beaumont called. In the next moment she came through the door. "That was the hospital. Your father's been hurt."

Allison shot out of the chair. "Is he okay?"

"Where is he?" B.J. asked at the same time.

"He's suffered some burns and smoke inhalation, but they couldn't tell me how serious it is. He's at the University Hospital." Her gaze slipped quickly over each of them. "Do you girls want to come with me?"

"I do," Allison said.

"I'll come too." Lisa slipped an arm around Allison's shoulders. "For moral support—but, um, I'll need to wash up and borrow some clean clothes."

"B.J.? Jennie?"

B.J. had an odd expression on her face. "N-not right now. Someone should stay here."

"I'll stay too." Jennie wanted to go, to check on the victims and learn who they were and how badly they were injured. She had a feeling, however, that B.J. needed moral support too—maybe more than her sister.

Mrs. Beaumont tossed them a disapproving look but didn't argue. "All right. I'll call as soon as I learn anything."

B.J. didn't respond.

When they were gone, Jennie bounced off the bed. "I need a swim." She grabbed B.J.'s arm. "Come on. It'll make us both feel better."

"What makes you think there's anything wrong?"

"I know. You're worried sick about your dad. This whole thing is eating you up inside. Just like it is me."

"I . . . I should go, but I can't. Not yet." Fear shone in her eyes. Through a bizarre set of circumstances, B.J. hadn't known her real father or her sister and stepmother until just a few months ago. B.J. and Allison's real mom had left Mr. Beaumont and Allison while she was newly pregnant with B.J. She never told Mr. Beaumont about the pregnancy and never told B.J. about her real father. When B.J.'s mom died, the birth papers revealed she had a family. With a chip on her shoulder as big as Texas, B.J. had reluctantly come to Portland to live with them. She was just now beginning to adjust.

"I'm not sure what's wrong. Maybe—" B.J. looked down at her hands. "I just found my dad, Jennie. I don't want to lose him."

Jennie nodded. "Let's swim a few laps to calm down. Then I'll drive us to the hospital."

If B.J. didn't need the exercise, Jennie did. Swimming laps helped her to relax and put things into perspective.

While she swam, Jennie wondered what would happen to the three hundred students who went to Trinity. They certainly wouldn't be able to use the building. Would they send them off to other schools or rent space somewhere? What would happen to their sports program and their weekly newspaper?

Gavin, the paper's editor, would be devastated. He loved journalism. Jennie wondered where he was. Knowing Gavin, he'd be right in the middle of things—probably on the scene, taking photos and interviewing people. Or he could have been at the school working on the paper. He often stayed after school. She imagined him trapped inside the inner room of the graphic-arts department, flames engulfing the walls, blowing out the windows.

Jennie hit the wall of the pool and came up for air, shaking the water from her hair and the images from her head. The phone rang. She pushed herself onto the deck. B.J. was still swimming and apparently hadn't heard the phone—or didn't want to.

Grabbing a towel, she hurried into the kitchen and answered with an out-of-breath hello.

"Jennie? Is that you?" Mom sounded upset, which meant she'd probably heard about the fire.

"Yeah. What's up?"

"The hospital just called me." She hesitated. "About Michael. They've been trying to find his family and . . . he still had me listed to call in an emergency."

"Is he—?"

"It's bad, Jennie," Mom interrupted. "They don't know if he's going to make it."

3

"The nurses felt someone should be with him," Susan McGrady said. "Since he doesn't have family close, I . . . I need to go. I'm leaving Nick at Kate's. Either you or your dad can pick him up on your way home."

Thinking of Nick brought another bout of pain. Jennie's five-year-old brother had just started kindergarten and loved it. There would be no school tomorrow or the next day or the next. . . . Jennie pushed the disappointing thought away and forced her attention back to her mother's request.

"You want me to get Nick right away?" Jennie explained about Mr. Beaumont being injured and her planned trip to the hospital with B.J.

"That's fine, honey. Go to the hospital first. Kate said he could stay as long as we need him to. I'll have your dad pick him up on his way home."

Jennie rubbed the goose bumps on her arms. "I'll see you at the hospital, then." She hung up the phone and leaned against the wall.

Jennie closed her eyes, feeling helpless and uncertain. Less than an hour ago she and Lisa were happy and comfortable and life was just about perfect. School had started after a long and exciting summer. She had looked forward to her classes and to settling down to her studies and taking care of Nick. Since she was part homeschooled, she did most of her work at home and came to school to check in with her teachers and to work on projects that could only be done at school.

Some of the kids thought the plan sounded complicated, but Jennie liked it. Mom had set up the program a few years ago so Jennie could care for Nick while Mom worked. Neither Jennie nor her mom wanted Nick in day care, so the homeschool/private school thing seemed ideal. Only now she might not have a school to go to.

As if the fire weren't enough, Jennie's intuition kicked in, giving her warning signals of even more trouble.

"Who was on the phone?" B.J. pulled the towel from her hair and flicked it at Jennie.

Jennie stepped aside. "Mom. Michael's been hurt really bad."

B.J. bit into her lower lip and wrapped the towel around her shoulders. "I guess it's time to go to the hospital."

Jennie's gaze dragged across the tiled floor, lingering on the drops of water still dripping from their wet suits. "Yeah. I guess it is."

Borrowing clean clothes—white cotton shorts and a tank top—from B.J., Jennie ducked into the outside bathroom and finished toweling off. She slipped bare feet into her white sandals, and after pulling her damp hair into a ponytail, she grabbed her book bag and waited for B.J. in the entry.

The St. John's Medical Center sat high atop what some Portland residents referred to as Pill Hill.

The waiting room, with so many familiar faces, reminded Jennie of the narthex after church with members milling around talking with one another. Only today there were no smiles, just dazed faces of people not quite ready to accept the tragedy as their own. Mrs. Talbot's husband had both elbows on his knees and his head buried in his hands. His wife was the school secretary. Jennie swallowed hard, thinking she should talk to him. She started toward him, but the receptionist called his name and he went to the desk.

"Our moms are over there." B.J. nudged her forward.

Susan McGrady was sitting next to Mrs. Beaumont against the far wall.

"I can't believe it's taking so long," Mrs. Beaumont said as Jennie and B.J. approached.

Both women looked up at the same time. Mom stood and gave Jennie a hug.

"Thanks for coming, B.J.," Mrs. Beaumont said, not getting up.

Mom hugged B.J. "Allison and Lisa are down in the cafeteria with Gavin. He was asking about you."

"Have you seen Michael yet?" Jennie asked.

"Just for a minute—to let him know we're here for him." Tears gathered in Mom's eyes and Jennie turned away. She wondered how Dad would feel about Mom's being so concerned for Michael. *He'd understand*, she told herself.

"Can I see my dad?" B.J. asked.

Mrs. Beaumont shook her head. "They're working on him right now. I only got to see him for a minute. He's doing okay. Said to tell you he loves you."

"It'll be a while before we can see any of them," Mom said. "Why don't you join Allison and Lisa. If we hear anything we'll have you paged. There's really not much point in all of us waiting here."

"Do you know who else was hurt?" Jennie shifted her gaze to the man still standing at the reception desk. "Mrs. Talbot?"

Mom nodded. "She was injured before the explosion. Um . . . something fell on her. She's one of the people Michael brought out."

"How bad?"

Mom shook her head. "They aren't telling us much yet.

Probably because they don't know for certain."

"Let's go." B.J. turned and nearly ran from the room, down the hall, and to the elevators they'd ridden up on.

Jennie leaned back against the wall next to the elevators. "I still can't believe any of this is happening."

"Yeah." B.J. punched the button for the ground floor. "I know what you mean. It's like a bad dream. Only we can't both be having it."

The elevator stopped and the doors opened. Having been there several times before, Jennie led the way down the corridor to the cafeteria.

They picked up drinks and headed for a table by the window, where Allison, Lisa, and Gavin were engrossed in conversation.

"Hey, Jennie." Gavin pulled out the chair beside him with one hand and pushed his glasses back against the bridge of his nose with the other. "What took you guys so long? Figured you'd be here long before this."

"I had other things to do." Jennie set her drink on the table and sat down.

"So were you there? Did you see it?" B.J. hooked a chair from another table and sat at the end between Allison and Jennie.

Gavin nodded. "I was in the journalism room working on this year's schedule, filling in deadlines for the newspaper and yearbook when I smelled smoke. I figured it was the furnace. Philippe still hasn't gotten the knack of working that thing. I thought I'd better check it out, but when I went to call, the line was dead. I didn't think too much about it 'cause there was no alarm. Figured if there was a fire there'd be an alarm, you know?"

Gavin paused to take a sip of his drink.

B.J. whistled. "No alarm. No phone. That's pretty weird."

"No kidding," Gavin agreed. "I went down to the office

to use the phone in there. Made it as far as the hall when . . . *Boom!* Good thing I got out of the room or I would have been dead meat."

"You weren't hurt?"

"A few bruises on my backside . . . guess I lucked out."

"I'm surprised you're here," Jennie said. "Thought for sure you'd be down there gathering all the facts."

"Couldn't. Soon as I got out of there, the EMTs checked me over and put me in an ambulance with some of the others that weren't as badly hurt." He shook his head. "It was the weirdest thing. The fire must have wiped out the electrical system."

"Or someone disabled it before setting the fire," Jennie murmured.

"Arson?" Gavin's eyes narrowed into slits. "No way." He ran his fingers up and down his glass, wiping off the condensation. "Is that what they're saying?"

"*They* are saying nothing of the kind." Allison leaned back. "No one knows for sure."

"Allison's right." Jennie wrapped her long braid around her finger. "I shouldn't have said anything. It's too soon to speculate."

"Maybe, but now that you mention it, having the phone dead and the fire alarm not working . . . that's just too much of a coincidence."

An hour later, Jennie's rear end was getting numb from sitting on the hard plastic chair. Her brain had shut itself off and she was operating on automatic pilot. They were down to four, Gavin having left twenty minutes earlier when his mom came by to pick him up.

Jennie nibbled on one of Lisa's cold French fries.

"You should eat something, Jennie," Lisa said. "Do you want me to get you a salad or something?"

Jennie looked at the limp fry and grimaced. "I'm not hungry." She glanced at her watch. Six-thirty. They still hadn't heard anything from the trauma center. "Think I'll go up and see what's happening. Anyone want to go along?"

Lisa stood. "I'll go. Um . . . maybe you could take me home pretty soon. Rafael is coming by at seven for his tutoring session." Lisa was working with Rafael on his English. "I could call him, but . . ." She glanced at Allison, then B.J. "You guys don't mind, do you? I know I said I'd keep you company, but I didn't think it would take so long."

"No, that's fine," Allison said. "We'll probably head upstairs pretty soon too."

B.J. glared at her sister. "You don't have to answer for me, Al. What makes you think I plan to stay?"

Jennie could have beaned her. Sometimes B.J. didn't have the manners of a pig.

Allison's head drooped as she stared at something on the table. "I'm sorry." Her head came up again as her gaze met her younger sister's. "You're right. It's your choice. I'd like you to stay with me, but if you want to go I'll understand."

After a long moment B.J. settled back in her chair. "I'll stay."

"Honestly," Lisa said when they were out of earshot. "B.J. can be such a brat."

"True. But she's having a pretty rough time with this. Think about how you'd feel if it was your dad that had gotten hurt."

"You're right. Speaking of dads, mine's due home tonight. I can hardly wait to see what he brought me." Lisa's father was a commercial pilot.

"Where'd he go this time?"

"China. And Hawaii. He's been gone for a week."

Reaching the elevator, Jennie pushed the up button. "You don't seem very excited for him to come home."

"I am. It's just that I'm a little nervous. Rafael's coming

over and . . . Dad hasn't met him yet."

"So . . ."

"So, Rafael is Hispanic."

"Does Uncle Kevin have something against Hispanics?"

Lisa shrugged. "I hope not. Mom says I shouldn't worry, but after what Mr. Beaumont said . . ."

"What?"

"Well, it wasn't what he said to me, exactly. It's what he told Allison and B.J. when Rafael first came."

The elevator doors swished open, and Jennie waited until they were inside before prodding Lisa to go on.

"He said Allison and B.J. were absolutely forbidden to see Rafael socially."

"Because of his race?"

"Apparently. That and the fact that they're on entirely different social levels."

"I can't believe . . ." Jennie stammered. "I thought Mr. Beaumont . . . I mean, he's sponsored Rafael's whole family."

"All I know is that he threatened to send Rafael back if he so much as caught Allison or B.J. even looking at him."

"Has Mr. Beaumont said anything to you?" Jennie held her stomach as the elevator rose three floors.

Lisa shook her head. "No, but I'm not so sure he knows. It's no wonder Rafael was so reluctant to ask me out."

Jennie tucked the information away. She'd think about it later. Right now she had to brace herself for news about Michael and the others.

Mom was sitting with Mr. Talbot this time. Lisa took a chair across from them and Jennie slumped into the chair next to her. "What's going on? Where is Mrs. Beaumont?"

Mom nodded toward the double doors. "In there. The doctor said she'd be able to take him home. He's got second-degree burns on his hands and arms and suffered some smoke inhalation. Otherwise, he's okay."

"Wish I could say the same for Elsa." Mr. Talbot sighed.

"She isn't . . ." Jennie couldn't finish.

"She's in surgery," Mom said. "Having a hip replacement. She fractured her hip when she was knocked down."

"That's the worst of it," Mr. Talbot said. "There were some other injuries too . . . bruises mostly. I'm just thankful Michael was there to bring her out before the fire got to her."

"How is Michael?"

"I still haven't heard."

Jennie watched a man in blood-soaked scrubs come through the doors and glance around the room. His gaze settled on Mom. "I have a feeling we're about to find out."

"Mrs. Rhodes?"

Jennie winced. She didn't like being reminded of how close Mom had come to being Mrs. Rhodes. "She's not—"

Mom stood up. "I'm Mrs. McGrady. Mr. Rhodes is . . . a friend. How is he?"

The doctor looked at Jennie and Lisa and frowned. "Are either of you relatives?"

"Michael is our youth director," Jennie told him. "Is he going to be okay?"

"I'm afraid not. We'll do all we can for him, but he has first- and second-degree burns on over seventy-five percent of his body."

"Oh no!" Mom covered her mouth and closed her eyes.

"Maybe you'd better sit down." He reached around Mom for a box of tissues and handed it to her. "Does he have any relatives? We should contact them."

Mom dabbed at her eyes and blew her nose. "He has a sister Ashley. She's a missionary in Tanzania. I don't know how to reach her. He should have letters in his apartment." Her gaze shifted to Jennie. "I don't have a key anymore."

"It's okay. We found a set on him. I'm sure the police will find it for us."

Beside her, Lisa sniffled and reached for a tissue. Jennie didn't cry. She just looked at the blood on the doctor's scrubs. Michael's blood.

4

"Can I see him?" Jennie heard herself ask.

"Soon. He's being transferred to the burn unit. It's on the fifth floor. I'd wait for another hour so the staff can get him situated. He'll be in isolation. It's important to keep his environment sterile. I'd suggest you come back around"—he glanced at the clock on the wall beside the reception desk—"eight or so."

Mom wrapped an arm around Jennie's waist. "We should go home. Your dad and Nick will want dinner. We can come back later."

Twenty minutes later Jennie and Lisa pulled into Lisa's driveway. Rafael was leaning against an older model Cadillac that looked like it had seen too many accidents and not enough paint.

"Hi," Lisa greeted as she stepped out of Jennie's car. "Sorry I'm late. Did you hear about the fire?"

"I heard." He brushed a hand through his course black hair and came toward them. His dark eyes had a brooding look that Lisa called mysterious. To Jennie he seemed sullen and angry most of the time. She could understand her cousin's attraction, though. Rafael was one great-looking guy.

"I was worried about your uncle," Jennie said. "Was he . . . in the building?"

"Sí, and Carlos."

"They're okay, aren't they?" Lisa wrapped her arms around his waist and leaned back to look at his face. His arms closed around her in a lukewarm welcome. At five-feet ten he was nearly a head taller than Lisa. They were a study in contrasts—Lisa's fair complexion and smattering of freckles on her face and arms; his bronzed skin, made even darker by working long hours in the sun. His sleeveless white muscle shirt did what it was supposed to do.

"No, they are not *okay.*" Rafael spoke in broken English. "Philippe try to put out the fire. Carlos is burned as well."

"I'm so sorry." Jennie didn't remember seeing family members in the hospital waiting room and said so.

"They were not badly hurt so taken to Sunnyside." He shrugged. "They will survive, but the burns are not the problem." He dropped his arms to his side.

"I don't understand," Jennie said.

"The polícia think the fire was not an accident. They blame Philippe."

"Oh no." Lisa stepped back and glanced at Jennie. "How could they? Jennie, we've got to do something!"

"There is nothing you can do. My uncle admits to being in the basement when the fire started. He tells them it is his fault." Rafael slipped his hands in the pockets of his cutoffs and dropped his gaze to the ground.

"That's terrible. Does he have a lawyer?" Lisa asked.

Before Rafael could answer, the door to Lisa's house swung open. "Jenny," Aunt Kate waved, "don't leave without Nick."

"He's still here? I thought Dad was picking him up."

"No. He called about half an hour ago. He'll be late. Something to do with the fire."

"Does Mom know?"

"Yep. She just called." Kate hesitated a moment, then said, "Jennie, could you come in for a minute? There's something I'd like to speak with you about."

Jennie didn't like the tone in Kate's voice or the strange look on her face. Something was wrong. Had Dad been hurt? She mumbled a hasty "See you later" to Rafael and Lisa and hurried inside.

"What's going on? It isn't Dad, is it? Please don't tell me he's been hurt."

Kate draped an arm across Jennie's shoulders. "No, your dad's fine." Leading her into the living room, Kate asked Jennie to sit down. "What I wanted to talk to you about is your mom."

"Mom?" Jennie dropped onto the sofa and grabbed one of the stuffed floppy-eared bunnies that served as cushions. "What about her?"

"Have you noticed anything odd about her behavior lately?"

"No." Jennie started playing with her hair again. "Not really. Have you?"

"Yes. She seems so tired and run down. And . . . depressed, maybe. I'm wondering if she's working too hard. With you back in school and on the swim team and Jason back home—I'm not suggesting your dad is a burden or that you're not doing your share, but when you think about the extra laundry, meals, picking up . . . all I know is that when your uncle Kevin is gone, there is a lot less work to do around the house."

Kate chuckled, her dark eyes shining. "Don't get me wrong. I dearly love him. I guess what I'm trying to say is that I'm worried about Susan." She shrugged. "Maybe she's just having a bad week. You haven't noticed anything?"

Jennie rubbed her forehead where she was starting to get a headache. "I haven't paid that much attention. I guess I have been pretty busy lately." Jennie's gaze moved from the floor to her aunt's face. Jennie and her aunt Kate shared many of the same features and were often confused for mother and daughter. They had the same dark hair and deep blue eyes. Not unusual when you considered that Kate and Jennie's father were twins. "You don't think she's sick or anything. . . ?"

"I hope not. With remarrying your dad and all, I expect she's had a lot to deal with emotionally as well as physically. I probably shouldn't even have mentioned it. It's just that when she brought Nick over today she seemed so drawn and . . . frail. She'd been crying."

"About Michael. She told you about his getting hurt?"

Kate nodded. "Yes—that poor man. Losing your mother and now this."

Jennie bit her lip. Worry sat like a big lump in the pit of her stomach. "Maybe it's not just because he's hurt. Maybe she's sorry she broke up with Michael to marry Dad."

"Oh no, honey. Susan loves your dad very much. She's concerned for Michael. That's only natural. No, I'm sure it's just stress and overwork."

Jennie sighed. "I hope you're right. Now that Mom and Dad are back together again, I don't want anything to mess it up. I'll try to do extra work around the house."

"I'm sure she'd appreciate that." Kate smiled and patted Jennie's hand. "Oh, and don't tell your mother I said anything. She seemed rather touchy the other day when I mentioned her looking a bit peaked."

"Right." Jennie stood. "I'd better get home."

"Kurt and Nick are in the backyard." Kate stood, too, and gave Jennie a hug. "Sorry to put this on your shoulders, honey, but I thought you should be aware."

Jennie nodded. "It's okay, Aunt Kate. Really."

Only it wasn't okay. The last thing Jennie needed was to be reminded of her mom's weird behavior. Jennie went to the back door and yelled for Nick to meet her at the car. She should have waited for him, given him a bear hug, and carried him to the car. At the moment, though, she didn't feel like hugging anyone. Normally she would have asked him about his day at school and looked over his papers, praising his work. Normally she would have been happy. Only today was not a normal day. The world seemed to have gone berserk, spinning out of control.

Jennie said good-bye and escaped to her car. Hot and stuffy as it was, it gave her something to hold on to. Something tangible and solid. She swatted at a mosquito flying near the dash and killed it. She draped her arm over the steering wheel and rested her head against it while she watched Lisa and Rafael go inside and Nick and Kurt come out. Kurt was five years older than Nick, but not much taller. They were more like brothers than cousins and did practically everything together. Just like she and Lisa used to.

That had changed too. Jennie wasn't much into boys. She did have a boyfriend, Ryan Johnson, but he lived at the coast next to Gram, and she didn't see him all that much. Which was okay. She had no intention of getting serious about guys yet anyway. Jennie's future plans included college, then law school. After that she'd think about marriage and babies. Maybe. The thought didn't excite her like it did some girls. But that was probably because she'd been helping her mom take care of Nick for five years. Not that she minded. She just didn't plan on having kids of her own until she was at least thirty.

She watched Nick run to the car and fumble with the door handle, finally managing to pull it open, climb inside, and close it again. She started the car while he whipped his seat belt on and gave her a wide grin that faded when she didn't return it.

"You mad at me or sumpin'?" He dumped his papers and book bag on the floor in front of him.

"No. I'm just sad today."

"'Cause of the school?"

"Partly."

"I'm sad too. Kurt says it's a 'venture and he hopes we won't have to go back to school at all for a whole year. But I don't want to not go to school. Do you, Jennie?" Nick's big blue eyes were nearly the same color as hers and their dad's and Kate's. It was a McGrady trait. So was the dark hair and being tall and thin.

"No."

"What do you think will happen?"

"I don't know." Jennie glanced at him. "Look, Nick. I don't want to talk about it, okay?"

" 'Cause it makes you more sad?"

"Yeah."

"Can I read you a book?" He reached forward and withdrew a chapter book from his bag.

She nodded. "Sure." Nick's *reading* usually took the form of him looking at the pictures and telling his own made-up story. He flashed her another grin and this time she returned it. His story would take both their minds off the tragic fire, and her mind off Michael and Mom.

She half listened as Nick recited the story about the Little Mermaid.

Jennie pulled into the driveway a short time later, relieved to see Dad's car parked in front of the garage next to Mom's. They were sitting in the front porch swing talking. Jennie's heart did a somersault—at least that's what it felt like. She loved seeing them together like that. Her fears about them splitting up subsided. Nick raced up the walk, dodging Bernie, his St. Bernard pup, and dove on top of them. Jennie watched her parents make a fuss over his drawings, feeling just a little jealous at being too old for that sort of thing.

"I can read, Dad!" Nick petted Bernie, who was still woofing, licking, wagging his tail, and being a nuisance.

"I'll bet you can." Jason McGrady scooted his son to his lap, both their dark heads bent over the book he'd been pretending to read to Jennie.

"Dinner's ready," Mom said, making no move to get up. "Nothing fancy. Just salad."

"Do you want me to bring it out here?" Jennie asked. Aunt Kate was right. Mom looked tired and thinner and there were dark rings under her eyes. Even her beautiful red hair looked different, not as full or shiny.

"That would be wonderful, Jennie. Thanks." Mom gave her a wan smile and leaned her head against Dad's shoulder.

They ate Chinese chicken salad with sesame seeds and crisp noodles, and herb bread on trays. Mom and Dad stayed in the swing, while Jennie stretched out on the chaise lounge and Nick sat in his small wicker rocker. For the first time since she'd heard the sirens that afternoon, Jennie began to relax.

At seven-forty-five, Mom heaved a heavy sigh, gave Dad a kiss, and got up. "If we're going to see Michael, Jennie, we'd better get going. I'd like to at least get these dishes in the sink before we leave."

Dad picked up his tray from the floor where he'd set it. "Are you sure you need to go again tonight? You both look exhausted."

"I'd like to check on him, darling. If he had family here it would be different. But he's alone and . . ."

Dad nodded, drawing a hand down his face. "Go ahead, then. Nick and I will take care of the dishes, won't we, little buddy?"

"Yep." Nick grasped his dad's hand. "Me and my dad will do it."

Outside Michael's room, a nurse helped Mom and Jennie suit up in isolation garb—a special cap and booties, and a gown and sterile gloves.

"Have you ever seen a burn patient before?" the nurse asked.

Mom said she had once. Jennie said no.

"It isn't a pretty sight. We have most of the deep burns covered, but you'll be able to see some on his face and upper torso."

"Is he in a lot of pain?" Mom asked.

"Unfortunately, yes. But it's the less severe burns that hurt the most. With the more severe burns, the nerve endings are gone."

"The doctor said he might not make it."

"That's true. The most dangerous thing right now is fluid loss and infection. We'll do our best."

Mom nodded. "Earlier, I told the ER people to get in touch with his sister, Ashley. Have you been able to contact her? Does she know?"

"I don't think anyone has been able to reach her yet. Is she his only relative?"

"I'm afraid so."

"Can I go in now?" Much as she wanted to see Michael, Jennie dreaded the visit and wanted to get it over with.

"Sure." The nurse opened the door and led Jennie inside. "You can talk to him, but don't touch him or anything around him. You can visit for about five minutes. I'll be right outside if you need me."

"Hi, Michael." She hesitantly approached the bed, swallowing back a pear-sized lump in her throat. "It . . . it's me. Jennie." Seeing Michael tore a hole in Jennie's heart. It was all she could do not to run out of the room screaming. Draped in white linen, he resembled a corpse. What she could see of his face was raw and blistered. She'd never seen anyone in so much pain or so badly burned. She took a deep breath to hold back the nausea, then focused on the call button beside his bandaged hand.

"Thanks . . . for coming, Jennie," he said in a raspy voice. "Means a lot."

She nodded. Tears streamed down her face and into the

mask. She sniffled but couldn't wipe them away for fear she'd contaminate the sterile gloves.

"Don't . . . cry." He raised his hand a fraction of an inch, then let it fall back on the sheets. "I'll be okay. I'm either—" he gasped, then went on in halting phrases, "going to make it through this . . . or I'll get to see God." Jennie watched his chest rise and fall several times before he spoke again. "Either way . . . I'll have it made."

Jennie wanted to ask him about the fire, how it started and if it was an accident, but talking seemed too painful for him. Instead she said, "I'll pray for you and get all the kids to pray too. Please try to get well, Michael. We need you."

When Michael didn't answer, Jennie moved her gaze up to his shoulder and past the excoriated cheek and nose to his eyes. His warm hazel eyes, glazed and unseeing, seemed to look right through her. She backed away. "Please, God, no. Don't let him die," she whimpered. "Please don't let him die."

5

Jennie ran from the room, pulling off the face mask. "I think he's . . ." She covered her mouth and closed her eyes, then slumped against the wall in the hallway.

"Oh, honey." Mom reached for her. Jennie pushed her away. She didn't want that. Didn't want anything but to get as far away from there as possible. Ripping off the gown and cap, she took off. "I'll be in the car."

"Jennie, wait . . ."

Minutes later, Jennie leaned against the car door. She'd forgotten that Mom had driven and still had the keys in her purse. Hard as she tried, Jennie couldn't stop crying. She pressed the heel of her hands against her eyes to dam the tears. "It isn't fair," she murmured. Michael was one of the kindest people she'd ever known. He didn't deserve this. She tipped her head back and raked her fingers through her hair. Looking at the stars, she gritted her teeth. "Why, God? How could you let this happen?"

She turned around and kicked the tire. "Ow." *This is stupid. Stupid. Stupid. Stupid. You're sixteen years old, for Pete's sake. Why are you acting like such a baby?* Four months ago she hadn't even liked Michael. Now her heart ached as though she'd lost a best friend. Jennie's mind whirred back to when she first met Michael Rhodes. Mom had known him from church and started dating him. With Dad missing for five years and presumed dead, Mom had decided to get on with her life, but that decision couldn't have come at a worse time.

In her heart, Jennie knew Dad was alive. She just needed to find him. Eventually she did, but he couldn't come home and she was sworn to secrecy. Dad worked for the DEA and had gone undercover to protect his family. She couldn't tell a soul—not even Mom. In the meantime Mom, thinking Dad had died, filed for a divorce so she would be free to marry Michael. Jennie hated the idea but eventually came to accept it. She'd even grown to love Michael. Then Dad showed up, and he and Mom fell in love all over again. Their story would have made a great novel. Except novels had happy endings.

She'd wanted Michael to find someone else and fall in love and be happy. Now he'd never have that chance. Even if he'd survived, his life would have been miserable. The fire had burned off half his face. Jennie shook her head to dispel the image. Maybe it was better that he did die.

Jennie placed her hands on the hood and leaned over the car, hauling in long, deep breaths. *You have to get control of yourself, McGrady. You can get through this.* She straightened again, determined not to fall apart. She shivered and rubbed at the gooseflesh on her arms. The hot day had turned into a cool night, and she hadn't thought to bring a jacket. Maybe she should go back inside.

Jennie brushed away the last vestiges of tears from her cheeks with the back of her hand. Hearing footsteps, she glanced up.

"Jennie? Are you okay?" Mom approached with a what-am-I-going-to-do-with-you look.

"I guess."

"I know seeing Michael like that was upsetting, but I don't appreciate your running off. What were you thinking?" Mom pulled the car keys out of her handbag.

Jennie lowered her head and stared at the faded white line

that separated their Oldsmobile from a teal-colored van. "I'm sorry. It's just . . ." She scrunched her eyes together. "He looked so awful. I've never seen anybody die before."

"Oh, honey." Mom wrapped her arms around Jennie. "Michael's not dead. Is that what you thought?"

"But his eyes . . . they were all glazed over and . . ."

"He's on high dosages of pain medication. If you'd taken a minute to check him, you'd have realized that."

"Oh." Jennie stepped away. "Mom, I feel so stupid and mixed up. I guess I should be happy he's still alive, but I was just thinking maybe it would have been better . . . Never mind. Are you ready to go?"

"I'm not going home, Jennie. Someone needs to be here with Michael. He is still alive, but his situation is critical. He may not last the night."

"Why do you want to stay? How can you stand to watch him?"

Mom looked back at the hospital, silhouetted against a red and purple evening sky. "All I know is that if it were me lying in that bed, I wouldn't want to be alone."

Jennie nodded. "I guess I'd feel the same way. How will you get home?"

"I'll call when I'm ready."

"What about Dad?"

"He'll understand." An odd look passed across Mom's face. Jennie half expected her to qualify her statement with an *I hope*. But she didn't.

Heading home, Jennie plugged a LeAnn Rimes tape into the tape deck and sang along with a remake of an old Righteous Brothers tune. She almost succeeded in blocking the images of Michael from her mind.

By the time she pulled into her driveway, Jennie wished she'd stayed with her mother. She could understand why Mom had chosen to be with Michael. What she couldn't understand was the way her stomach hurt at the thought of telling Dad.

Jason McGrady was sitting in the family room watching a news program. Jennie came up behind him and wrapped her arms around his neck. "Hi. Nick in bed already?"

"Yep. Glad you're back." He looked toward the entry and frowned. "Where's your mother?"

"Still at the hospital." At his puzzled look, she added, "Michael's really bad and Mom felt like someone needed to stay."

"What about the pastor or some other church member?" He rubbed the back of his neck.

Jennie shrugged. "No one else was there. She said you'd understand."

He stood and dug his hands into the pockets of his faded jeans. "Did she want me to pick her up later?"

"She said she'd call." Wanting to change the subject, Jennie asked, "Have you heard any more about the fire—I mean whether it was arson or not?"

"No." The frown slipped from his face and he lowered himself back into the chair. "We won't know for certain until it cools down enough to investigate."

"How long will that be?" Jennie straddled the arm of the sofa.

"Not sure. Twenty-two hours maybe."

"Do they have any idea how it started? Or where?"

"No. Probably the furnace room."

"Have you ever worked on an arson case, Dad?"

"Not directly, and I'm not working on this one. Neither are you."

"I wasn't—"

"Then why all the questions?"

"I . . . never mind." Jennie jumped up and stomped into the kitchen.

Mom would have yelled at her to adjust her attitude. Dad

ignored her. Jennie didn't know which was worse. She fixed a snack of brownies and milk, took a helping to her dad, who grunted an insincere thank-you. He'd changed channels and was watching a baseball game. After a few minutes of feeling about as wanted as a skunk, she mumbled something about having homework.

"Jennie!"

She stopped halfway up the stairs and turned around. "What?"

He came up beside her, dragging his hand through his hair like he so often did. "I'm sorry. I'm upset and I shouldn't be taking it out on you."

"Are you mad at Mom?"

He hesitated. "Not exactly." His gaze met hers. The scar on his cheek curved as he smiled. "At any rate, I'm sorry."

Jennie hugged him. "That's okay. Do you want me to stay down here and keep you company?"

"If you want. I was about to shut off the television. Have to appear in court tomorrow so I thought I'd better go back over the case."

Ordinarily Jennie would have asked him what the case was about, but not tonight. It was only nine-thirty, but all she wanted to do was take a hot shower and go to bed. "I'll see you in the morning, then."

Something cool and wet touched her hand. Jennie pulled it back under the covers. "Bernie, go away." The St. Bernard pup nudged her again. "You're not supposed to be in the house."

"You gotta get up, Jennie." Nick tugged at her blankets. "Somebody needs to take care of me."

"Where's Mom?"

"I don't know. And Daddy's gone too."

Bernie whimpered, then let loose with a loud bark.

Scenes from the previous day drifted back to her. The fire. Michael. The burn unit. Jennie lifted her head and peered at her digital alarm. Seven.

Nick pushed at her shoulders. "Come on, Jennie, we have to get ready for school."

Jennie groaned and rolled over onto her back, rubbing the sleep from her eyes. "There is no school today, Nick."

"Why? Is it Saturday? It can't be Saturday 'cause yesterday was Monday and—"

"No. It's not Saturday." She patted the bed. "Come up here. We have to talk."

Nick climbed up on the bed and straddled her stomach. "What do you want to talk about? You better make it quick."

Jennie closed her hands around his skinny arms. "Remember what happened yesterday? Why Mom took you over to Aunt Kate's?"

His bony shoulders rose and fell under his green plaid pajamas. "All she said was she needed to go to the hospital to see somebody that was real sick."

Great. Mom hadn't told him about Michael. "Right. Do you know why the people were at the hospital?"

"Yeah. Kurt says they got burned in the big fire. And the school got burned and the church and everything."

"Right. And that's why we can't go to school."

"Why?"

Jennie heaved an exasperated sigh. "Because of the fire. The school burned down."

"But, Jennie." Nick's wide blue gaze met hers head on. "They got it all fixed already."

"No . . ."

"They do. I saw a picture of it on telebision—on the news."

"Oh." Understanding dawned. "That was probably a picture of what it used to look like."

"Uh-uh." Nick wagged his head back and forth. "They builded a new one."

Jennie lifted him off to the side and scooted off the bed. "Go get dressed and put Bernie out."

Surprisingly, he didn't argue.

Jennie hurriedly braided her hair and threw on shorts and a T-shirt. She didn't know if it was the right thing to do, but having Nick actually see the place was going to be the only way to convince him. Besides, she needed to see Trinity for herself. She could understand why it would be hard for Nick to comprehend the damage. She had a hard time believing it herself.

In the kitchen, Jennie read Dad's hastily scribbled note. *Jennie and Nick. Sorry to rush off, but I had some important business at work. See you at dinner. Dad.*

After a quick breakfast of yogurt and cereal, Jennie called her mother at the hospital. When Mom finally got on the line, she asked about Michael.

"He's about the same. Is your dad there?"

"He left already. Do you need me to come get you?"

She didn't answer for a moment, then said, "Why don't you come at ten. Reverend Cole said she'd try to spell me. She agrees we should try to have someone with Michael all the time."

"Maybe I could take a turn," Jennie volunteered. "Since we probably won't be going to school for a while. . . ."

"That's sweet of you, honey. I'll put you in the schedule."

By the time she hung up, Jennie felt better. Sitting with Michael wouldn't be the most pleasant task, but at least she'd be giving her mother a break. And Dad wouldn't need to get upset.

At eight-thirty, Jennie turned up the familiar hill to the school and parked at the top of the driveway. Yellow police tape had been strung between barricades. A security guard leaned against his car watching her. A fire engine and a lone fire fighter stood at the ready near the burned-out building in case fire erupted again.

"How come you're stopping here?"

"The police won't let us go any farther. Besides, we'll be able to see the whole school yard from up here."

Jennie couldn't count the number of times she'd turned into the drive and been greeted by the brilliant blue-tiled roof. She exited the car and came around to help Nick out. Picking him up, she carried him to the side of the road. The bitter smell of smoke and burned wood nearly choked her as she made her way to the ledge. About thirty feet below them the once beautiful structure lay in ruins.

Nick took one look and buried his face in her neck. "I want to go back home. I don't want to be here."

Jennie wished she hadn't brought him. Her gaze swept across the black debris. The only thing left standing was the gymnasium, and that only because it was a separate building joined to the rest of the complex by a covered walkway. The walkway had collapsed. She closed her eyes, remembering the way it had been only the morning before—the roof proudly shimmering in the sunlight like peacock feathers. The building had been built in four stages. The church formed the central-most part of the fan-shaped structure. Members had built it twenty years before. Five years later they added the grade school and day care.

Five years after that they built an expansion on the opposite side of the church to add the high school. And only two years ago they'd built the gymnasium and covered the entire complex with the new blue roof.

Jennie opened her eyes again. Her gaze settled back on a couple patches of blue that hadn't been blackened by soot. "Well, at least it's not all gone," she said. "Look, Nick. The gym is still there." She pointed to the far end of the property.

"And the playground equipment is there too."

He lifted his head from her shoulder. "Can we go swing?"

"Not yet. It'll have to be cleaned."

He sighed. "Oh."

"It won't be so bad," Jennie went on, wanting to wipe the despondent look from his face. "Pretty soon workers will come and clear all the ashes and burnt stuff away. Then they'll bring in lumber and start building. They'll have big bulldozers and trucks and we can come and watch sometimes."

His eyes brightened. "Will they make it just like it was? And will it have a library?"

Jennie nodded. "Sure." Though she said the words, she wasn't certain she quite believed them. It would take millions of dollars to rebuild and replace what the fire had destroyed. She thought about the artwork in Michael's office and the stained-glass window in the sanctuary. The Bibles and the hymnals, the thousands of books that lined the shelves of their library.

She had to get out of there before she started crying again. As she turned away, a movement near the woods behind what used to be the chemistry lab caught her eye. Jennie focused in on the lone figure in army fatigues creeping along the tree line. Crouching down, he ran past the playground equipment and disappeared behind the gym. The cap he wore kept her from seeing his face or making a positive ID.

Jennie had heard somewhere that a criminal always returns to the scene of the crime. She wasn't sure if that was true, but one thing she did know. That guy had no business being there.

6

Jennie put Nick back in the car. "Stay here for a minute. I gotta check on something." Jogging over to the security guard, she reported what she'd seen.

"You sure?" The guard, obviously irritated with her for causing him trouble, scanned the grounds. "I don't see anyone."

"He went behind the gym. He might be trying to break in."

The guard crossed his thick muscular arms, and for a minute Jennie thought he might not take her seriously. Then, apparently deciding he'd better check out her story, he unhooked a cell phone from his belt and punched in a code. After a moment's hesitation he said, "Yeah, this is Chuck Owens. Some kid down here says she saw a guy snooping around the school. I doubt it's anything, but I better check it out." While he talked, he headed down the steep drive.

"Aren't you going to wait for backup?"

He cast her a frosty glare and kept going. Jennie walked back to her car, where she had a better view.

"Can we go home now? I want to see Mom." Nick leaned out the window.

"In a minute."

"Why can't we go now?"

"Because somebody's down by the school who shouldn't

be there, and I want to find out who they are." *Besides*, she thought to herself, *the guard might need help.*

Nick settled back in his seat, arms crossed and a scowl on his face. Below her, the guard walked to the far end of the grounds near the woods, then moved back toward the gym. He went behind the building and several minutes later came to the front entrance and went inside. Jennie shook her head. Not a smart thing to do.

A squad car pulled up behind her. An officer jumped out. Hand close to his weapon, he approached her. "I'm Officer Cooper. Got a call from a security guard saying he got a tip there might be trouble—know where he went?"

"He's in the building." Jennie quickly filled him in.

"Did the man you saw have a weapon?"

"I didn't see one. But if I'd been the guard, I wouldn't have gone in there without backup."

A second officer drove up before Cooper could respond. He was just getting out of his car when the door to the gym flew open. The man in fatigues ran out. He was no longer wearing a cap.

"That him?"

"Yeah." Jennie's heart ripped into overdrive. The guy looked straight at her. Jared Reinhardt.

Cooper and the other officer drew their weapons and at the same time shouted for him to stop.

For a second Jared looked like he was going to run. His gaze darted back to the building, over to the trees, and back to the police.

"Put your hands up where I can see them," Cooper yelled.

"Don't shoot!" Jared lifted his hands.

Within seconds the police descended on him, making him lie face down while they frisked him. They yanked him to his feet, pulled his hands behind his back, and cuffed him. After talking with him, the second officer went inside—probably to find the guard. Cooper walked Jared up the hill and ordered him into the back of his squad car.

Jared didn't speak to her, though his cheeks were flushed with anger. She had no doubt his menacing stare was meant to silence her, but Jennie had no intention of being intimidated. She met his gaze head on.

"Do you know him?" the officer asked.

"Not very well. His name is Jared Reinhardt. He's a . . ." Jennie looked back at Jared. He looked more frightened now than angry. She wished she could ask him what was going on. Had he told her the truth of wanting out of the gang? If so, why was he at the school? Had he been responsible for the fire?

"Was he a student here?" the officer prodded.

"No. Michael, our youth director, had been counseling him. Jared told us he was a skinhead and wanted out of this neo-Nazi group he'd been with."

The guard and the officer emerged from the building.

"Good, he's okay. I was afraid . . ." Jennie let her voice trail off. She felt a strange sense of relief, not only that the guard was unhurt but that Jared hadn't harmed him.

"Jennie!" Nick whined. "Please, can we go home?"

"In a minute." Jennie pushed her strange mix of feelings aside and focused on what the officer was saying.

"I need to know how to get hold of you," Cooper said.

"Sure." She gave him her name, address, and phone number.

"McGrady . . ." Cooper mulled the name over. "Jason McGrady's girl?"

"Right."

He nodded and flashed her a grin. "Good man. Looks like we won't have any trouble getting hold of you if we have any more questions."

"Guess not." Jennie opened her car door but didn't get

in. Concern for Jared still loomed large in her mind. "Officer Cooper?"

He looked up from his notes. "Yes?"

"Um—what will happen to Jared?"

"Depends. He claims he didn't know the area was off limits. Says he left something in Michael's office and came here to see if it survived the fire. Wouldn't tell us what it was, though."

"Could you let me know whether you decide to charge him or not?"

"Sure." He raised an eyebrow. "Say, he's not your boyfriend, is he?"

"No. Just curious, that's all."

Jennie ducked into her car, wishing she could forget about the strange attachment she felt toward Jared all of a sudden. She didn't like it in the least. Didn't especially like *him*. He stood for everything she hated. Jared had been running with a band of white supremacists. Likely the same gang that had beat up a man only last week because he was a Jew. She shuddered at the thought.

Jennie started her car and eased away from the wide shoulder onto the road. She had the oddest sensation of being drawn into Jared's life. "You're losing it, McGrady," she mumbled.

"What are you losing?" Nick asked.

Glad for the diversion, Jennie grinned. "Nothing important." *Just my mind*, she added to herself. "How would you like to go visit Aunt Kate and Uncle Kevin? We have about an hour before we need to pick up Mom."

"Yay!" He bounced up and down. "I get to play with Kurt! I get to play with Kurt!"

Jennie grinned. It sure didn't take much to make Nick happy. She wished she could switch moods that easily.

"Kate, Kevin, Kurt, and Lisa. Kate, Kevin, Kurt, and

Lisa." Nick chanted the names six or seven more times. "Jennie?" Nick stopped bouncing.

"What?"

"Did you know all their names start with a K except for Lisa's? How come they didn't name her with a K too?"

" 'Cause she was named for Grandma Calhoun, and her name is Lisa May."

"Well, they shoulda named her Karen, then they could've had four Ks. Now they only got three." He giggled and began chanting the names again.

"That's enough, Nick."

"Why?" Nick's blue gaze drifted up to hers.

"Because I said so." She softened her tone. "I'm not in a very good mood right now, so I need you to not talk for a few minutes. Okay?" She caught his hand and squeezed it. "Why don't you sing me a song instead."

He shrugged. "Okay. Ummm. How about the li'l monkeys jumpin' on the bed?"

"Good." While Nick sang about the monkeys falling out of bed and bumping their heads, Jennie thought about Jared and his skinhead friends. She remembered seeing films from the old south where men would hide behind white gowns and hoods, killing and maiming blacks in the name of justice. It was the same justice many early settlers used in dealing with Native Americans. And that Hitler and the Third Reich had used against the Jews. They were all different groups that fell under one ugly word—prejudice.

Jennie shook her head, surprised at how far afield her mind had drifted. Funny how thinking about one thing could lead to another and another. Jared Reinhardt, skinhead, neo-Nazi/white supremacist. Prejudice.

Though she didn't want to jump to conclusions, Jennie couldn't help wondering if the fire had been race related. Of course, the authorities hadn't said for certain if it was arson. All she'd heard so far was speculation.

Jennie ended up leaving Nick at Kate's and bringing Lisa along with her to the hospital. They arrived at quarter to ten. Since Pastor Cole hadn't come in yet, Lisa offered to stay with Michael while Jennie took Mom home. Lisa had already donned the isolation garb and gone inside. She sat next to the bed, talking with Michael, and didn't seem at all affected by his appearance.

Jennie waited for Mom to come out of the room—her very tired-looking mother. Jennie frowned, noticing how much weight Mom had lost. She had been dieting off and on, trying to keep her weight down since she'd been pregnant with Nick. She sure didn't need to worry about losing weight now.

"You look terrible," Jennie said when Mom joined her just outside the room.

"Thanks." Mom lifted her shoulder-length auburn hair off her neck.

"You've lost weight."

"I have?" She smiled as though it were a good thing. "I haven't even been trying."

"Mom." Jennie peered into her mother's eyes from her six-inch height advantage. "I'm not sure it's a good idea for you to stay here so much."

Mom looked away. "I . . . I have to do this, Jennie. I don't expect you to understand, but—"

"You don't still love him, do you? I mean—you married Dad and . . ."

Mom pulled off the paper shoes and stuffed them in the garbage, then slowly removed the gown. Her blouse looked rumpled. "I'm not sure how to answer that. I do love Michael—not in the same way as I love your father, of course, but . . ." Mom's gaze met Jennie's again. "He was my best friend for six months. You can't just turn that kind of thing off."

Mom picked up her sweater and handbag. "You don't have to worry about me, honey. I'll be fine."

"I hope so." Jennie started for the elevator. "You ready?"

The elevator doors opened like curtains on a stage. It wasn't the elevator itself but the person inside who brought the analogy to mind.

The Reverend Marissa Cole stepped out in a flurry of autumn colors—red, brown, cream, and gold. "Susan, Jennie. I am so glad I caught you." Her hands fluttered as she spoke, showing off her slender fingers and long nails. Each nail had been painted a different color to match her dress. "I apologize for being late. What with the press and the police, I'm lucky to be here at all."

As usual, Jennie found it hard not to stare. Whether she meant to or not, Reverend Cole demanded attention. Jennie marveled at the way the brown in her floor-length dress perfectly matched her smooth bronzed skin and deep chocolate eyes, while the tawny gold matched her very short hair. Even her voice matched, Jennie thought. If voices had colors, Marissa's would be ivory—like silky cream. Though she was born in the United States, Marissa had lived in South Africa for the last five years as a missionary. Prior to that, she'd traveled with a Mercy Ship. As a result, she was an exotic blend of culture, style, and personality.

"The police? What did they want?" Mom asked.

"They're questioning everyone who was in the building when the fire broke out. You never heard so many questions." Marissa sighed heavily and adjusted the strap of a huge brown leather bag over her shoulder. "But let's not talk about that right now. How's our patient?"

"I wish I could say he's doing better, but there's been no change. Lisa Calhoun is with him right now."

"Oh good. In that case, I'll run down to the cafeteria and grab a bite to eat. Believe it or not, all I've had today is coffee."

Jennie believed it. Marissa Cole had a Tigger personality, all bouncy and bright. This morning, though, she seemed bouncier than usual.

"Would you two like to join me?" Marissa asked.

"I'd love it. I haven't eaten this morning either." Mom turned to Jennie. "You don't mind, do you?"

"I guess not." What could she say? Actually, she did mind. She was hoping to talk to Gavin. If anyone knew the latest news on the fire, he would. On the other hand, Marissa had just spoken with the press and the police. Jennie tagged along behind them, half listening as Mom filled Marissa in on things she needed to know about Michael.

While Mom and Marissa ordered breakfast, Jennie helped herself to a glass of orange juice, told the cashier her mom was paying for it, and secured a table by the window. Marissa's strong alto voice carried all the way to the seating area. Mom's didn't, which was why Jennie heard only one side of the conversation. Enough to know they'd changed topics.

"The Lord works all things for good," Marissa said. "And this is no exception. That fire was a terrible tragedy, but do you know, people from all over the country are responding with donations? We'll be able to rebuild in no time."

"Has the board met at all to decide what to do in the meantime?" Mom asked as they approached the table and sat down.

"Oh yes. We met last night. As you know, we didn't lose the gym. Praise the Lord for that. A lot of smoke damage, but it'll be as good as new in a week. We'll set up temporary offices there and hold services."

"And the children?"

"That's a problem." Marissa used the pads of her forefinger and thumb to carefully pry open a container of jam. "Mr. Beaumont has some space in one of his plants. He's downsizing. It would take some fixing up, but we might be able to work something out. Otherwise we'll have to integrate the students into other schools."

"That would be terrible," Jennie said. "You can't just split us up. We—" She stopped, realizing it would do no good to protest. Their school was gone.

"I know," Marissa cooed. "It's a terrible thing. But we don't have many options. If by some miracle we got the funding to rebuild tomorrow, we couldn't move into the school until next year."

"What about portable classrooms? Once the rubble is cleared out—"

"It would be too expensive." Marissa hesitated, then added, "But I'll suggest it. You never know."

"I think we'll go to homeschooling completely," Mom said. "At least for Nick. There'll be less disruption that way. It'll probably be best for you, too, Jennie. You wouldn't be able to be on the swim team, but the pool will still be here for you to practice, and maybe next year . . ." Mom held her stomach. "Um . . . I'm not feeling so well. Excuse me." Covering her mouth with her hand, she pushed back her chair and fled.

"Do you want me—" By the time Jennie got to her feet, Mom was already halfway to the rest room. Jennie turned to Marissa. "I'd better go check on her."

The toilet flushed as Jennie entered the rest room. Looking pasty white and shaky, Mom emerged from the stall. "I'm all right, Jennie. Just lost my breakfast is all. You didn't need to come in."

"Maybe you should see a doctor. There are lots of them around."

Mom wet a paper towel, squeezed the excess water out of it, and pressed it against her forehead, then each cheek. "Don't be silly. I probably shouldn't have had eggs. They haven't been setting too well with me lately." Mom looked into the mirror, where she met Jennie's concerned gaze. "All right. If it will make you happy, I'll see a doctor. But not today. I'll call Dr. Cameron and set up an appointment. Now, go back and keep Marissa company."

"You sure you're okay?"

Mom assured her again, telling her she'd be out in a few minutes. Though reluctant, Jennie did as she was told.

"Is everything all right?" Marissa asked when Jennie came back.

"Mom says it is, but I'm not sure."

"You think she's lying to you?"

"No. But I don't think she's telling me everything." Jennie picked up her napkin and tore off the corner. "My aunt is worried about her too. I mean, what if Mom is really sick? Maybe she's got a disease and doesn't want to tell us."

Marissa's warm brown gaze softened as she patted Jennie's hands. "Your mother seems to be a wise and caring lady. I'm sure if there was a problem—especially anything as serious as all that—she'd tell you."

"Not necessarily." It wouldn't have been the first time Mom had kept a secret. Back when Dad was missing and presumed dead, Mom had been seeing Michael for several months before she decided to let her family know.

"It does no good at all to worry, Jennie. You need to trust your mother. But more important, you need to trust God to work everything out according to His purpose."

Marissa's words had meant to comfort. They did anything but. If God would allow Trinity to burn to the ground, Jennie wasn't certain she trusted Him with her mother.

7

"What am I thinking?" Mom ran her hands through her already mussed hair. "We forgot to pick up Nick." Jennie and Mom had just pulled into their driveway after being at the hospital.

"I was hoping you wouldn't notice. Don't worry about it. I'll go over there right after I get Lisa and visit Michael."

"That's sweet, honey." She yawned. "I could use some sleep."

"And don't worry about dinner tonight. I'll take care of it."

"Well, that is nice. Thank you."

After telling her mother again to get some rest and not to worry about Nick, Jennie headed back to the hospital.

Flipping on the radio and not wanting to hear a commercial, Jennie punched the buttons until she found a song she liked by Vince Gill. *I Still Believe in You.* She sang along until it ended.

"More of your favorite tunes to come," the DJ promised. "But first an update on that church fire."

Jennie turned up the volume.

"Police are questioning several people today in conjunction with the Trinity fire, now believed to be arson. Five people were injured in that blaze. One, Michael Rhodes, still remains in critical condition."

"So it *was* arson," she said aloud. And one of the people they were questioning had to be Jared. "I wonder what he was looking for." Maybe she could ask Michael.

Once in Michael's room at the hospital, she told him what had happened that morning and asked if Jared had brought him something.

"Yes." Talking seemed painful for him and Jennie wished she hadn't asked.

"If it hurts too much, you don't need to answer. I'm sorry. I just wish I knew if he was telling the truth. About anything."

"I . . . believed . . . him," Michael rasped.

Jennie pulled her chair a few inches closer. "Can you tell me what he brought you?"

"Box. Didn't have . . . time . . . to look."

"It was in your office?"

"Yes." He hesitated again for a long time. "Need to tell you . . . in case . . . I . . . don't make it."

"Oh, Michael, please don't talk anymore." It twisted Jennie's insides to watch him struggle so. "You'll make it. I know you will."

"Jared was . . . turning . . ."

"Miss McGrady?" The nurse came into the room. "We need to change Michael's dressings now. You'll have to step out."

Jennie glanced back at Michael. "I'll be back as soon as they're done."

Lisa was waiting when Jennie stepped out of the room. "Well?"

Jennie told her what Michael had said about Jared. "Looks like he was telling the truth about giving Michael something."

"Okay, but what did he give him?"

"And why did he want it back?" Jennie thought of something else. "Michael said he didn't have time to look at it. Probably because of the board meeting. That means Jared was at the church close to the time the fire started."

"Oh wow. He could have done it. We need to tell the police."

"Not yet. I want to hear what else Michael has to say." Jennie glanced around. "Where is Reverend Cole?"

"Talking to the police again." Lisa sighed. "She never did get in to stay with Michael this morning."

"She isn't a suspect, is she?"

"No. At least I don't think so."

Jennie swung her gaze back to the curtained area where the nurses were working on Michael. "They might be a while. Do you know where Marissa is?"

"Visitors' waiting room."

"Let's go."

Jennie and Lisa slipped into the crowded room. Reverend Cole sat in a corner chair, looking like a foreign dignitary. Her subjects, mostly reporters along with a couple of police officers, hung on her every word. "There is no doubt in my mind who set that fire." Marissa rearranged the folds of her skirt. "I have been getting threats since I came on staff three weeks ago. Trinity was targeted because of me and the people I brought with me. Though Trinity is not a predominantly black church, since my arrival our numbers have tripled and are growing every week."

"So you see this as a racist crime," one of the reporters said. "And you know who is responsible?"

Marissa seemed in her element. "Racist, yes—a hate crime through and through. There are people in this world who would like nothing better than to destroy the black community. You know who I'm talking about. The Northwest has a large white supremacist contingency that openly admits to wanting to eliminate races other than their own. Why, only last week they held a convention on a compound they purchased in eastern Oregon." She shuddered. "Folks out there parading around in their white robes and hoods . . . you all saw them."

Marissa sat up straighter and lifted her chin in an even more stately pose. "I have a message for the people behind this. You can burn our churches. You can maim or even kill our bodies, but you cannot destroy our spirits. We've lost our beautiful building, but the building is not the church—the people are. We will rebuild. We will continue to stand together, united. And one more thing," Marissa's voice softened. She looked straight into the camera. "I want to challenge every one of you to join us at Sunday services."

The room erupted in questions. "Reverend Cole," a woman nearest Jennie asked, "how can you issue an invitation like that? Aren't you angry with them?"

"I am angry about what they have done. I am not angry with them as individuals. They like sheep have gone astray."

"I suppose the next thing you're going to tell us is that you love them." The man who spoke wore a cynical expression.

Reverend Cole's gaze drifted downward, then up again. "No," she said softly. "I am sorry to say that I can't profess to love them. I am much too human for that. And my own personal wounds are too deep. But I know that God does love them—just as He loves all of his children. God is willing to forgive and to love much more readily than I. Eventually He will work that spirit of love and forgiveness into me and into all the people of Trinity who have been hurt by what they have done."

Reverend Cole went on to tell them about God's grace and love and how repentance—turning away from sin—could save the soul. She'd turned the waiting room into a chapel and the press conference into a sermon. Maybe that was why Pastor Dave and Michael had urged the board to hire her.

"You said your own wounds were too deep. Can you tell us what you meant?" a reporter across the room asked.

Marissa pursed her lips, and for a moment Jennie thought she might not answer. "When I was a little girl some men came to our home. My daddy had been called to testify against a known white supremacist who was standing trial for the murder of our neighbor—a man who was running for mayor. The police chief assured Daddy that our family would be protected."

Marissa's lovely brown eyes drifted closed. She touched her colorful fingertips to her forehead and drew them down her cheek. "I believe now the chief may have been a secret member of the Ku Klux Klan. The night before the trial, four men in robes and hoods beat and hung my daddy from the oak tree in our front yard. Then they beat and killed my mother. The police never even found a suspect."

In the stillness of the room, Jennie could almost hear the beating of her own heart. In the awkward moments that followed, no one seemed to know what to say.

Marissa drew in a deep breath. "I find it very hard to love those people. But God was good to me. He placed me in the home of a wonderful family who gave me all the love I could possibly want. They raised me as I believe my parents would have. To be bold and to speak my mind and . . . to do the will of God."

"Have any provisions been made for the children to continue school?" someone asked, obviously wanting to change the subject.

Marissa gave them the same answer she'd given Jennie and Mom earlier.

"Are you aware the police are holding the janitor for questioning?"

"No." She threw up her hands in disgust. "Poor Philippe. He would never do such a thing. He and his son, Carlos, have only been in this country for two months. He is thrilled to have found work. No, I do not for one moment believe he set that fire. To find the real culprits, I suggest the police turn this town upside down and bring in everyone who's ever had an affiliation with the white supremacists."

An urgent message over the intercom drowned out her last words. "Code Blue. Code Blue. Emergency staff report to the burn unit immediately."

Jennie's heart sank, landing somewhere near her feet. *Please, God, don't let it be Michael.* The operator repeated the message several times as Jennie and Lisa made their way back to the unit. Half a dozen doctors and nurses poured into Michael's room.

"What's going on?" Lisa asked. "Why aren't they suiting up?"

"They don't have time." Jennie grabbed Lisa's arm and pulled her back out of the way. "He's coding."

"Coding—you mean his heart?" Eyes wide and teary, Lisa sank into the chair at the nurses' desk.

Jennie stood behind her, absently massaging Lisa's neck and shoulders while she watched the flat line on the monitor above their heads.

8

"God, please let Michael live," Jennie whispered. Behind closed lids she imagined Michael getting out of his bed and walking toward her. He stood in the center of a white light.

"I have to leave now," he said. "God is taking me home."

No. You can't—not yet. Jennie wanted to argue but stood transfixed, unable to speak.

"I wanted to finish working with Jared. God has great things planned for him. He needs a friend, Jennie, to help him through this. I'm counting on you." In the next instant he was gone.

Jennie opened her eyes. "He's dead." The words tumbled out of her mouth before she could stop them.

"He can't be." Lisa pointed to the monitor. "Look! His heart is beating again!"

"What?" Jennie could hardly believe it. The image she'd seen and heard seemed so real. She couldn't have imagined it. Could she?

A nurse came out of Michael's room shaking her head. "We should have let him go."

"Couldn't," a second nurse said, stripping off her gloves. "He didn't have a living will. You know that."

The first nurse turned on the water and began washing her hands. "Sometimes we go too far."

Jennie tuned them out, confused by what had just happened.

"Why did you say that, Jennie?" Lisa asked. "Why did you say he was dead?"

"I—never mind." She couldn't very well tell anyone what she'd seen. Not now. What she thought had been God bringing her a message must have only been her imagination. "I didn't think he'd make it, I guess." She sighed, thinking she should be rejoicing and thanking God that Michael hadn't died. Only she didn't feel thankful—just sad.

One by one the team of doctors and nurses that had responded to the code drifted out of the room. Through bits and pieces of conversation, Jennie put it all together. Michael was now on life support—a ventilator that would breathe for him. They'd stabilized him—for now.

Reverend Cole had come in during all the excitement. Now she was getting into the isolation garb so she could take her turn staying with Michael. It seemed a shame Marissa had to cover up her beautiful outfit. The pale green scrubs did nothing for her rich brown skin.

"How long can you be here?" Jennie asked.

"Until two. I'm meeting with the board at two-thirty."

Jennie nodded. "I'll be back. Or Mom will."

"I wish Marissa could stay longer," Jennie said to Lisa on the way back to the car. "I have something I need to do and Mom looked so tired. I don't want to wake her up."

"I could come back this afternoon," Lisa said. "I kind of like being here, watching the nurses and reading to Michael."

"Really?"

Lisa's lips separated in a wide smile. "You don't need to look so surprised. Remember when we did those career-guidance tests last year?"

"Yeah."

"Nursing was one of the careers I scored highest in." She wrinkled her nose. "I thought I'd be too squeamish, but I did okay."

"Much better than me." Though Jennie had some medical knowledge and knew CPR, she had no desire to go into a medicine-related field.

"Maybe I'll be a forensic pathologist and you can be a detective and we can solve murders together."

Jennie chuckled. "I'll believe that when I see it. Sitting in a room with a patient is a whole lot different than doing autopsies."

"Hmm. You may have something there. Guess I should think this through a little more."

While Lisa thought, Jennie opened her car door and scooted inside. The day was another scorcher. Temperatures, according to the weather report on KISN, would reach ninety degrees. It was hotter than that in her car. Definitely a day for air conditioning.

"Do you want me to go back to the hospital this afternoon?" Lisa asked when they were only a short distance from her house. "You didn't say."

"That would be great. I need to check something out."

"What?"

Jennie pinched her lips together. Releasing a deep sigh, Jennie told Lisa about her strange vision—or whatever it had been.

"Wow." Lisa frowned. "Wow," she said again.

"It was so weird. I wish I could forget about it, but—"

"You can't. What if it's a message from God?"

"If that's the case, why is Michael still alive?"

Lisa frowned. "Maybe it's a sign of what's to come. Maybe God meant for Michael to die. You heard what that nurse said about going too far."

"Maybe. Even if it was only my imagination, I feel like I have to talk to Jared. He probably does need a friend right now. And I know it's what Michael would want." Jennie slowed to turn onto Lisa's street. "I wish I knew if I could trust him. I keep thinking about what Marissa said about the white supremacist groups. Even if Jared is telling the truth and does want out, the fact that he joined them in the first place . . ." Jennie shuddered. "It's hard to have sympathy for somebody like that."

"True, but Marissa also talked about forgiveness. If he does want out, we should support him and show him he's better off without people like that in his life."

"I know Michael believed in Jared, but don't forget, he was at the school just before the fire broke out. If he's innocent, why would he have come back this morning? I'm not sure we can trust him."

"I suppose you're right. What are you going to do?"

"Go to the police station. Find out if they arrested Jared. Then I'm going to try to talk to him myself."

Jennie pulled into Lisa's driveway. "Will you need a ride to the hospital later?"

"I don't think so. I'll leave a message on your answering machine if I do."

Jennie started to drive away, then remembered her brother. Lisa met her on the porch.

"Nick's not here, Jen. Mom left a note. She and Dad took the boys swimming out at Vancouver Lake. They won't be back until around four."

"Great. That gives me plenty of time to do some digging."

Driving to police headquarters, Jennie had mixed feelings about talking to Jared. The night before, Dad made it clear he didn't want Jennie involved with the investigation. He wouldn't like her involvement with Jared either. Maybe she should talk to him first—bring him up to date. Unfortunately, if she did that, he might forbid her to even talk to Jared again. Though she felt a strong obligation to Michael to help Jared, she didn't want to go against Dad's wishes. She hated situations like that.

Jennie found a parking spot a couple blocks away from the police station, plugged the meter, and hurried up the street. The morning had already escaped and Jennie hoped she wasn't too late. If Jared had been released, she wouldn't have a clue where to find him.

"Jennie!" Dad came out of the building just as she was going in.

"Hi." Jennie waited for him to join her.

"What brings you down here?" His smile faded. "It isn't your mother?"

"Mom's fine. Sleeping. Reverend Cole is at the hospital with Michael." Jennie dropped her gaze to the steps. "He coded, Dad. They have him on life support."

"I'm sorry to hear that."

"Mom doesn't know yet. She'll probably be mad at me for not waking her up, but she seemed so tired, I thought she should rest."

"Good decision, princess." He rubbed the back of his head. "Um . . . so why did you come down?"

Jennie thought for a moment before speaking. She briefly considered sidestepping the truth but doubted she'd get away with it for long. Besides, she had a lot of love and respect for her father and didn't want to destroy that.

"While you're deciding whether or not to be straight with me, how about some lunch? I'm starving."

Jennie flashed him an embarrassed grin. "How did you know what I was thinking?"

"A father knows these things." He draped an arm across her shoulders. "Lacy's Deli okay?"

"Sure." Jennie fell into step beside him and told him about seeing Jared that morning as well as what had happened in her encounter with Michael.

"That's quite a story." Dad opened the door to the deli and motioned her in. The deli had a large counter where people could buy baked goods and sandwiches and salads to go. It also had a seating area, which was usually overflowing. According to her father, the family-owned restaurant had the best food in town.

After being seated in a far corner in one of the six tan vinyl booths, Jennie said, "The reason I came down here was to find out what happened to him."

Dad scanned the menu and set it aside. "You're not developing feelings for this guy, are you?"

"No. At least not in the way you mean. I just want to help him, that's all—I mean, if he's telling the truth about wanting out." Jennie glanced up at the waiter, a youngish man with curly dark hair and a skull cap. Daniel Goldberg, the owner's son, greeted Dad and gave her a nod.

"Too bad about your school burning. Must be tough." He set two glasses of water in front of them and pulled out his note pad.

"Yeah. How did you know it was my school?"

"Mr. McGrady told me. You'd be surprised at the topics we can cover over a cup of coffee."

"What's good today, Daniel?" Dad asked.

"Mom made a great black bean chili. And we got a special on our Reuben."

"Sounds good. I'll have both—and coffee."

Jennie ordered a shrimp salad and iced tea.

"Okay. Be right back with your drinks."

"Nice kid," Dad murmured when he left.

"I guess." Jennie shrugged and took a sip of water. "So-o-o, you have any idea what happened to Jared, or how I can find out?"

"He was questioned and released."

"Oh."

"Remember what I told you last night about my not being involved in the case?"

"Uh-huh."

"Well, I was wrong. The chief turned it over to me this morning. I first got called in to question the janitor. He's a recent immigrant and speaks very little English."

Jennie nodded. "Philippe Hernandez. I met him and his little boy a few days before school started—over at the Beaumonts'. Philippe's brother Manuel—that's Rafael's dad—works for them. Mr. Beaumont got Philippe the janitor job at the school."

"Right. Beaumont has already set him up with a lawyer."

"You don't think he set the fire, do you? Rafael said he was a suspect."

"What I think doesn't matter. The poor guy's confessing to all sorts of things. It's like he's trying to blame himself."

Dad moved back when Daniel brought the drinks, then after waiting for him to leave said, "I have a feeling he's protecting his son."

"Oh no. Not Carlos. Dad, he's such a neat little kid." Jennie remembered a tragic fire a few months back where police discovered the arsonist was a little boy who'd been playing with matches. "Do you really think he could have done it?"

"I doubt it. Carlos couldn't have disarmed the fire alarm or the phone. We think that's what happened."

"I thought homicide didn't handle arson." Jennie stirred her iced tea.

"We're usually in on the investigation. You'd be surprised at how many people use arson to cover up a murder."

Jennie set her glass down and leaned forward. "Murder—is that what happened?"

Dad nodded. "Forensics found human remains in what used to be a small sleeping room near the furnace. No one seems to know who it is, or if they do, they're not talking."

9

Murder. Jennie's mind spun with possibilities. The fact that no one from church or school had been reported missing only added to the puzzle. Had the victim been the target, or suffered the tragedy of being in the wrong place at the wrong time?

Daniel brought their food and they ate most of the meal without speaking. Dad seemed lost in thought—and no wonder. Questions bounced around in her head like dozens of Ping-Pong balls.

"Jennie, I . . ."

"Was it . . ." They spoke at the same time.

"Go ahead." Dad waved his fork at her.

"The person in the fire—was it a man or a woman?"

Dad shrugged. "Don't know. We're thinking it may have been a vagrant who managed to find his or her way to the basement. We're checking all the members of Trinity, though, in case it's someone who lives alone."

"What were you going to say?" Jennie asked.

"Believe it or not, I was going to ask if you'd like to give me a hand on this case."

"What?"

Dad chuckled. "You heard me."

"Yeah, it's just—" She arched an eyebrow and gave him a skeptical look. "Dad, this is so out of character for you."

"I know. But you have connections that I don't. You've already met Hernandez and his family. All I want you to do is get close to Carlos. Make friends with him—let him play with Kurt and Nick. The boy knows something. I'm hoping you can get him talking. We've already called in a psychiatrist to work with him, but I have a hunch he'll open up faster with you and the boys."

"That won't do much good if he can't speak English."

"Unlike his father, Carlos can speak fluent English. He learned it in a Catholic missionary school in Mexico. But right now he's not talking at all—in any language. Philippe says he hasn't spoken since the fire. We figure he's experienced some sort of trauma—like maybe he saw the person who started the fire. In which case the arsonist might be after him."

"Like Sarah," Jennie mused, thinking back to one of the first crimes she'd helped to solve.

"Who?"

"A girl I met in Florida when I went to Dolphin Island with Gram in June. Sarah witnessed her dad's murder, and afterward she went into some kind of shock where she couldn't talk or even take care of herself."

"Like a catatonic state?"

"Right. She was like that for two years. The dolphins helped her come out of it." Jennie shuddered, remembering how the murderer had tried to kill both her and Sarah by trapping them in a cabin and torching it.

"Dolphins?"

"Yeah—there's this thing they do down there called dolphin therapy. Swimming with the dolphins helped Sarah remember. They are so cool, Dad. It's like they have this sixth sense."

"Dolphins." Dad shook his head. "I'm afraid we don't have the time or the money to ship Carlos to Florida to swim with the dolphins. And we don't have two years. Let's hope you, Kurt, and Nick will have a similar effect." Dad smiled, then turned serious again and said, "Since Philippe has confessed, we can't dismiss the possibility that he's telling the truth. We'll probably have to hold him. I . . . um . . . I told him we'd look after Carlos for a few days. Worked it out with social services. Poor kid doesn't need any more trauma. The psychiatrist agrees."

"That's a great idea, Dad. He can bunk with Nick." Jennie slid her plate to the side of the table. "What about Mom? We really should make sure it's okay with her. Having another kid around might not set too well with her right now."

"I'll talk to her. If she has a problem with it, I'll ask Kate. The important thing for Carlos is that he has people around him who care and who can provide some sort of stability."

"What about his family? Maybe it would be better for him to stay with Manuel and Rafael."

"It would, but there's no room. They've already got six people crowded into the two-bedroom guesthouse."

"What about the Beaumonts? They have more than enough room, and B.J. and Allison would love taking care of him."

"They might, but their parents wouldn't. I already talked to Beaumont. He doesn't want Carlos or Philippe anywhere near the property until this mess is straightened out."

"He really thinks one of them might be responsible for the fire?"

"There's still the possibility. After the fire, the nurses at the hospital found a book of matches in Carlos's pocket. Apparently he's fascinated with fire. Beaumont caught him playing with matches shortly after they came up from Mexico."

"Oh boy." Jennie sighed. She cast her father a curious gaze. "Maybe having him stay with us isn't such a good idea."

"Oh?"

"I guess I'm having a little trouble understanding how

you could put our family in jeopardy. I mean, what if Carlos did it?"

"We'll just have to make sure he doesn't get a hold of any matches."

"But, Dad . . ."

He wiped his mouth on a napkin and set it aside. "It's a remote possibility, princess, but not likely. My intuition tells me he's an innocent kid who witnessed a terrible tragedy."

"Then what about the arsonist? You said he might come after Carlos."

"I'm hoping no one will find out where he is. He'll be in protective custody." He drew his hands down his face. "Your mother will never go for it. I shouldn't even be suggesting—"

"Dad, I think it's the right thing to do. Mom will be okay with it—especially if we pitch in and help."

"Let's hope so. I'm bringing him home for dinner tonight."

On her drive home, Jennie's thoughts bounced around from Michael and Jared to Carlos. She shifted from being elated about her dad's request for her help to being disappointed about not finding Jared, and then to being excited about Carlos staying with them, and being worried about Michael. And back to Jared again.

Since the police wouldn't cooperate by giving her Jared's address, and since she hadn't seen him at the usual haunts around Pioneer Square, she'd had no luck finding him. Maybe she'd have to wait until he contacted her. And maybe she should just forget it.

You shouldn't be worrying about Jared, she told herself. *You should be concentrating on helping Carlos.* Maybe she'd take him and Nick and Kurt for a walk in the park. They could bring a ball and play catch. They could all go swimming tomorrow. The important thing, Dad had told her, was to make him feel comfortable and provide a safe environment.

Jennie pulled into her driveway at two that afternoon. “The first thing I’d better do is decide what to fix for dinner.”

The banging of pots and pans in the kitchen told Jennie Mom was up and that she was not in a great mood. “It’s about time you got here.” Mom slammed a small pan into a larger one and set them in the cupboard, then started in on the silverware. “Where have you been?”

Jennie opened her mouth and shut it again when Mom kept talking.

“I can’t believe you didn’t call to tell me about Michael. When were you planning to do that?”

“I didn’t want to wake you, and I figured there wouldn’t be anything you could do anyway.” Jennie hitched herself up on the stool at the counter. “How did you find out?”

“I called the hospital when I woke up.”

“I don’t see what you’re so upset about. You act like it was my fault he coded.”

“Don’t be ridiculous. I just want to know what’s going on.” Mom threw in the last fork and slammed the drawer closed. “If you’re willing to take care of dinner, I can still run over to the hospital this afternoon.”

“I told you before I’d fix dinner.” Jennie glanced at the clock on the stove. “Lisa’s there by now so you don’t need to go until—”

“It isn’t a matter of needing to go.” Mom glanced up at Jennie, her vacant gaze scanning the room. “Where’s Nick?”

“Swimming.” Jennie explained what had transpired that morning and got as far as lunch with her dad before noticing the pallor on her mother’s face. “Mom, I think you’d better sit down. You don’t look so good.”

“I’m fine. Just need something to eat, that’s all.” She

grabbed a banana from the fruit bowl and sank onto the kitchen chair.

"Can I get you anything? Some yogurt or cereal? Something to drink?"

Mom shook her head, intent on peeling the banana. The phone rang. Mom looked at it and then at Jennie. Jennie grabbed the phone on the third ring. "Hello."

"Jennie, is that you?"

Relief swished through her. She hadn't talked to her grandmother in way too long. "Gram, where are you?"

"Still in the Bahamas. We've decided to stay another week." Gram was a travel writer, and she and her husband, J.B., had gone to the Bahamas at the request of her publisher.

"Oh." The news disappointed Jennie. "I wish you could be here. Things are kind of crazy."

"Kate told me about Trinity and Michael. I'm so sorry."

Jennie filled Gram in on some of the details when Mom hurried away from the table, looking like she was about to throw up again.

"I'd better go." Jennie briefly explained her mother's odd behavior. "I wish I knew what was wrong. She's too sick to be worried about Michael, but he's all she seems to care about anymore."

"Has she seen a doctor?"

"Not yet. She promised to make an appointment, but I don't think she has."

"Hmm. Do you think it would help if I spoke with her?"

"Maybe."

Jennie took the phone into the living room, but the bathroom door was still closed. "Gram, I don't think Mom's going to be able to talk to you right now."

"I'll try to call her back later, okay? I'd have her call me, but we're on the road. Speaking of which . . . I've got to run, sweetheart. Tell your dad I called and give everyone a big hug from me. Love you."

"Love you too, Gram." Jennie held the receiver against her chest for a moment before hanging it up. She wished she knew what to do for Mom. Worried and frustrated, Jennie hung up the phone and made her way back into the living room. She knocked on the bathroom door. "Mom?"

When she didn't answer, Jennie called again. She heard a faint moan. Pushing down the rising panic, Jennie opened the door. Mom was lying in a heap on the bathroom floor.

10

"Why won't you let me call 9–1–1?" Jennie sat back on her heels beside the sofa where Mom lay.

"Absolutely not. I just fainted, that's all."

"Maybe I should call Dad, then."

"No. I'm feeling much better. I'm going to lie here for a few minutes, then I'm going to the hospital to see Michael." Mom handed Jennie the cool washcloth she'd put on her mother's forehead earlier.

"If you have the flu it isn't a good idea to go see Michael."

"I don't have the flu. I'm upset—too much stress, most likely."

Jennie cringed, partly because if it wasn't the flu it might be something more serious, and partly because of the extra burden of having Carlos there. "Mom, there's something I should tell you." She explained her father's plans to bring Carlos home. "I think it would be really neat if he could stay with us, but you won't hardly have to do anything. I'll take care of him and Nick. You won't even know he's here." Jennie heaved a sigh. "What am I saying? Maybe it would be better if he stayed with Aunt Kate or—"

"Nonsense. That poor child. Of course he can stay with us. It'll be difficult, but we can manage."

"Mom, are you sure? I thought with you not feeling good lately you might not want to."

"Oh, Jennie, I wish you wouldn't worry about me. We'll get through this."

Mom left half an hour later to go to the hospital. When she'd gone, Jennie pulled ground beef out of the freezer, deciding to make hamburger stroganoff—a family favorite. She prepared a fresh jug of lemonade and a pitcher of iced tea, then mixed up a raspberry gelatin dessert.

With the dessert made and chilling, Jennie went up to her room. Things had been happening so quickly since the fire, she hadn't had a chance to do much thinking about it. Then with Mom being sick and Michael hanging on to life by a thread, she'd been too worried to try to think about much else.

"It just doesn't seem real," she said aloud as she moved aside her stuffed animals to make room on her window seat. Jennie loved her room with its bay window and Victorian flavor. She sat in the warm afternoon light. Somehow she kept expecting to wake up and find she'd been having a terrible nightmare. Part of her felt numb, like her brain had been shot full of Novocaine. Another part felt like the Novocaine was wearing off. She didn't know what to do about Jared or if she should even do anything.

That afternoon when Dad had asked for her help, Jennie could hardly believe it. The thought of contributing something had left her feeling almost normal. She liked the idea of being involved in the case. Working with Carlos was a good start, but already she wanted more. The detective in her wouldn't rest until she learned the truth and the police had the person or people responsible behind bars.

"So where do I start?" *Where you usually start, McGrady,* she answered herself. *By writing it down.* Jennie retrieved a pad and pen from her desk and went back to the window. On it she wrote: *Trinity Arson Fire.* Using her usual format, she divided the page into four columns across labeled *suspect, motive, means,* and *opportunity.* Moving down the page she drew a line under the labels and started listing suspects. *Jared* took first position, then *Philippe.* And *Carlos.* Though Jennie thought it unlikely that either Carlos or Philippe had started the fire, it was too soon to rule out anyone. And Philippe had confessed.

Another possibility struck her as she wondered about the identity of the person killed in the fire. Why was he there? Had he started the fire? Or had the fire been set to deliberately kill him and cover up another crime? Under suspects she wrote a big question mark. There were so many unknowns, Jennie doubted she'd ever be able to figure it out. There had to be other suspects as well. Anyone in the building could have done it. On a fresh sheet of paper she began listing the people she knew were at the church. *Board meeting: Mr. Beaumont, Michael Rhodes, Reverend Cole, Pastor Dave, John Mossier, Charles Talbot.* There were a couple of other people she couldn't remember. Others who were at the church included Jared, Gavin, Philippe, Carlos, and Mrs. Talbot. She tapped her pen against her lip, wondering if she'd left anyone out.

Going back over the names, Jennie still felt the most likely suspect was Jared. Jared had both the means and the opportunity. He'd been at Trinity prior to the board meeting. He could have easily slipped into the basement, disconnected the wires, and started the fire. Under motive she wrote the word *hate.* Jennie found it hard to believe that people could actually murder someone or destroy a church because they didn't like the color of someone's skin or their beliefs or lifestyle. "But it happens," she said aloud, thinking about what Marissa had told them about her parents. "What I don't understand is why Michael believes so strongly in Jared's innocence."

The doorbell rang, putting an end to her musings. Jennie

tore down the stairs to answer it. Lisa stood on the porch with B.J. and Allison.

"I hope you don't mind our dropping by," Allison said. "We need to talk."

"No, come on in." Jennie stepped back to allow them to enter, then led them to the kitchen. "Um—you guys want a Coke or lemonade or something?"

"Sure, Coke would be great." B.J. hooked her leg over the barstool to watch.

The others opted for lemonade.

Lisa, as much at home at Jennie's as in her own house, took down glasses while Jennie retrieved the drinks from the refrigerator.

"Let's sit on the porch," Jennie suggested. "I haven't cleaned my room since before school started and I'm not sure I have much sitting space."

"No problem." B.J. lowered herself onto the lounge chair. Allison took the new white wicker rocker, curled one leg up under her, and set the rocker in motion with the other.

Jennie sank onto the porch swing and, once Lisa had climbed in, set it to swinging. "What did you want to talk about?"

"Al and I are working on a suspect list." B.J. set her drink on the floor beside her.

"We think maybe the arsonist may have been after Dad."

Jennie nearly choked on her lemonade. "Your dad? Why?"

"He's made a lot of enemies lately." Allison glanced at B.J. as if wanting her to take over.

"One of Dad's businesses has been having financial trouble. He decided to downsize, which meant laying off about twenty people. He's gotten some threatening letters."

"Did he tell the police?" Jennie asked.

"No. He says he doesn't think his employees would burn down his church to get even with him."

"He's probably right," Lisa said. "If they wanted to hurt your dad, it seems like they'd figure out something that wouldn't involve so many other people."

"Lisa's right," Jennie agreed. "Whoever torched Trinity was ruthless. I mean, burning down a church and school doesn't seem like a logical way to get revenge."

"Maybe, but people who lose their jobs sometimes get desperate. Remember the postal worker who went to that restaurant and gunned down a bunch of innocent people? The guy who fired him wasn't even there."

"And there was a man who went into the KOIN building and took hostages." Allison stilled the rocker. "I think we should check out Dad's employees. B.J. and I already started. So far we've talked to four—all of them have other jobs already and didn't seem all that upset. With the four of us working, we could get through the list much faster."

"I'll help," Lisa volunteered. "How about you, Jennie?"

She shrugged. "I guess we should consider the possibility of revenge. But we need to let my dad know. He's working on the case now." She told them about the victim burned in the fire. "The fire could have been set to cover up a murder."

Allison shuddered. "That's so awful." Tears filled her blue eyes. "Don't you just feel like you want to . . . I don't know . . ."

"Hurt someone?" B.J. finished. "I'd like to find whoever's responsible and beat them to a pulp." She clenched her fist.

"B.J., you shouldn't be making threats you can't follow through on," Allison said in her big-sister voice. "The best thing we can do is figure out whether or not someone in Dad's organization did it. I think the police should know, too, but not yet. I'll tell our dad about your father handling the case, Jennie. He might change his mind. If not, we'd better wait until we find some solid evidence. Dad would be furious if the police started hassling people—especially if they didn't do it."

Jennie didn't like the idea but agreed not to say anything for now. Allison reached into her canvas bag and retrieved some papers, then distributed them around. "We made up a list of employees from Dad's files."

B.J. tucked her hands behind her head and stretched out. "I figure you and Lisa can take the first half, and Al and I will take the rest."

Jennie had to smile at the way B.J. had linked up with her sister. Only a month ago she would have preferred anyone's company but Allison's.

Jennie looked over the names. The list included each person's position in the company and their addresses. "Any ideas on how we should approach these people? We can't very well ring their doorbells and say, 'Hi, I'm taking a survey. Did you burn down Trinity to get even with Mr. Beaumont?' "

"Get real, McGrady." B.J. guzzled down the last of her Coke.

"Wait a minute," Allison said. "The survey idea is good. We can develop a list of questions to ask. Like how long have they been in the neighborhood. Where they work, whether or not they go to church, what church they go to—that sort of thing."

"How did you handle the others?" Jennie asked.

B.J. shrugged. "We told them our dad was concerned about them and wanted to know how they were doing. Which is true."

"I like that approach." Lisa glanced at Jennie. "By showing concern for them—which is really the truth—we have a chance to get inside and talk to them for a while."

"Their immediate response will tell us if they're still mad at your father," Jennie said.

"True." Allison tipped her head to the side, letting her shimmering blond hair cascade forward. "The people we talked to thought it was so nice that Dad cared enough to check on them."

"Sounds good to me," Jennie said. "When do we start?"

"We'll probably hit a few tonight after dinner."

Jennie frowned. "I can't go tonight. Dad's bringing Carlos over. I'm supposed to be watching him."

B.J. grimaced. "I heard you were taking him in. Dad thinks Philippe is covering up for Carlos."

"What do you think?"

"I feel sorry for both of them," B.J. said. "Poor kid is scared spitless. So's his dad. Personally I think they're innocent, which is why we wanted to check out Dad's ex-employees."

Lisa shifted around, tucking her legs up under her. "Rafael says his uncle is an honest man. He's pretty upset that the police were so quick to take him into custody. He claims that Philippe's getting a raw deal because he's Hispanic."

"That's not true," Jennie said, jumping to her father's defense. "Dad has no choice but to take Philippe's confession seriously. He's trying to help."

"I'm just telling you what Rafael said. You don't have to get so upset." Lisa bit on her lower lip.

Jennie sighed. "Sorry. This whole prejudice thing upsets me. Rafael is wrong. No matter what nationality Philippe is, he'll be treated the same."

"By Uncle Jason, maybe, but . . . well, never mind. We need to decide when we can go out and check on these people." Lisa took a long sip of her drink, then leaned forward to set the glass down on the floor beside the swing.

"With Carlos being here and Mom not feeling well, I'm not sure when I can. Maybe tomorrow."

"I know!" Lisa exclaimed. "You could bring Carlos and Nick over to my house in the morning. The boys will want to play with Kurt. I bet Mom will watch them for a few hours." Lisa jumped out of the swing. "I'll call her right now. See if they're back from taking the boys swimming."

While Lisa called home, the others took their empty

glasses back to the kitchen, then went back outside to wait.

A few minutes later Lisa came out. "It's all set. She said she'd be glad to watch the boys. Oh, and, Jennie, she wanted to know when you were picking up Nick. No hurry, she just wants to know if she should set an extra plate for him for dinner. I told her I thought you'd probably come get him since Carlos was coming."

Glancing at her watch, Jennie winced. It was already five. "I'd better move it." To Lisa she said, "Are you going with them or do you want me to take you?"

"Might as well ride with you."

B.J. and Allison left, Jennie wrote a note for her parents, and Lisa called home to let her mother know what they were doing.

Jennie pulled into her driveway at six and began dinner, which wasn't easy with a five-year-old hanging on her leg. "What's that boy's name again, Jennie?"

"Carlos." Jennie pried him off and pointed to the refrigerator. "Go get me the mushrooms and an onion."

"How old is he?" Nick opened the fridge and nearly disappeared inside.

"Eight." Jennie pulled out the electric frying pan, turned it on, and dumped in the partly thawed hamburger.

Every time she answered one question, he came up with two more. "Why is he coming?"

"Because he needs a place to stay for a few days."

"Why?"

"Because he does."

"Can Kurt spend the night too?"

"Ask Mom."

"When's Mom coming home?"

"Soon. I hope." Growing impatient, Jennie hustled him out of doors to play with Bernie. Five minutes later he was back inside, so she put him to work setting the dining-room table.

Mom finally arrived while Jennie was stirring the mushroom soup into her hamburger, onion, and mushroom mixture. Nick transferred his attention to her, explaining in detail what Jennie had told him about Carlos. Mom didn't seem to mind his constant talking or his questions. She parked herself at the kitchen table and cuddled him.

"How are you feeling?" Jennie asked.

"Better. Wish I knew what was causing these spells. A nurse I talked with today said I might be anemic. I picked up a special vitamin supplement on my way home. Maybe that will help. And yes, I called to make an appointment with the doctor."

"Good. How's Michael?"

"No change, I'm afraid." She gave Nick another squeeze. A car pulled into the driveway. "Sounds like your daddy's home. Better go see."

Jennie, nearly as anxious to see Dad and Carlos as Nick, turned down the heat on the frying pan, stirred the noodles, and followed her mother and brother into the living room.

"Daddy, Daddy!" Nick squealed over and over as he ran to the front door.

"Hey, there's my boy."

Jennie smiled as Dad scooped Nick into his arms and swung him around, then gave Mom a kiss. Carlos, head down and looking frightened, stood just inside the door. Dad took Carlos by the hand and drew him into the room. "Carlos, this is my family—Nick and Mrs. McGrady, and you know Jennie." Dad pulled her into a warm hug, then turned back to his charge.

"Hi, Carlos." Jennie gave him a welcome smile. "Hope you're hungry. I made a big dinner."

Though he didn't say a word, his large dark eyes told her

he was glad to see a familiar face. The idea of dinner seemed to brighten his sad features.

Not wanting to be left out, Bernie stood just outside the door and barked. Dad introduced him to Carlos, and for the next few minutes before dinner Nick and Carlos sat on the porch petting Bernie and getting licked in return.

Later that evening, Jennie helped the boys get ready for bed and read to them. Carlos was beginning to respond to her but still refused to or could not speak. She knew it would take a while to earn his trust, but she couldn't help wishing he'd come around quickly.

Mom and Dad came up to tuck the boys in.

"Are you two ready for prayers?" Mom asked.

Carlos jumped up and ran to his bag. He held up a rosary and clutched the cross in his hand, fingering the beads.

"What's that?" Nick asked.

Dad explained the Catholic tradition of praying the rosary.

"Can we say that one for Carlos, Dad?"

"Sure. I don't know all of it, but we can say the Apostles' Creed and the Lord's Prayer. Then we'll let Carlos do the rest."

Dad said something in Spanish to Carlos and they all knelt around the bed.

Afterward, Nick recited his special prayer. "And dear God, please help my new friend Carlos to talk again and please help us be his friends."

With tears in her eyes, Jennie kissed both boys good-night and went downstairs. The dishes from dinner were still stacked in the sink, so Jennie went to work on them.

A few minutes later she heard voices in the living room. "I can't believe you're going out again tonight," Dad said, not bothering to hide his annoyance.

"Keep your voice down. I thought we already settled this."

"Honey, I have no problem with you visiting Michael once—maybe even twice a day. What I don't understand is this crazy notion that you need to be there all night. The man's an adult—he has nurses at his side around the clock. You, on the other hand, have a family."

"But he doesn't. I finally got word to his sister, and she'll be here in a couple of days. In the meantime I *am* his family, and I intend to be with him as much as possible."

"And I'm your husband, or have you forgotten that?"

"Jason, don't—"

"Don't what? You want me to pretend it doesn't bother me? I can't do that. I need you here, Susan. You owe me that much."

"I owe you?!" Mom's voice rose a couple octaves. "Jason McGrady, I don't owe you anything. You disappear from our lives for five years, without so much as a phone call, then you come back and expect me to be the dutiful little wife who bows to your every whim? I don't think so."

Jennie's heart felt tight. She could hardly breathe. *Please don't argue. Please,* she pleaded silently. Jennie squeezed her eyes tight and forced her hands deep into the dishwater, grabbing hold of the silverware and willing herself to concentrate on washing them.

"I'm leaving now," Mom announced. "I may or may not be back in the morning." The front door slammed with a finality that nearly jerked Jennie's heart out.

11

Jennie's hand stung. She looked down and gasped at the pink-tinged water. "Shoot." She pulled her hand out. Blood streamed from a cut on her forefinger. "I can't believe I did that."

"Did what?"

Jennie spun around, slinging pink soapy water all over his white shirt. "Oh, Dad, you scared me. I thought you were still—"

"What did you do to yourself?"

"I was washing dishes and cut my finger on a knife."

He snatched her hand and raised it to the light. "Doesn't look too bad." Grabbing a paper towel, he wrapped it around the wound and applied pressure to stop the bleeding. "Come sit down."

Jennie sank into a chair at the kitchen table. "It's just a little cut, Dad," Jennie said. "It'll be fine."

He unwrapped her hand and examined the cut. "Doesn't look like it needs stitches. You should be more careful. Didn't your mom teach you how to wash knives properly?"

Jennie bristled, resenting his attitude. "Dad, I *know* how to do dishes. I know I'm not supposed to put the sharp knives in the sink with the other silverware. It was an accident, okay?" She lifted her head and met his gaze, swallowing back her anger. It was the first time since he'd come home that she'd said a harsh word to him. "I . . . I'm sorry."

Dad's dark blue eyes shone with understanding. "You heard your mother and me arguing, didn't you?"

Jennie nodded.

"Just like old times, huh? We can't seem to be together for two minutes without a disagreement. Then I come and take it out on you."

"You're not going away again, are you? 'Cause I know Mom loves you. She's just worried about Michael. He's a good friend and—"

"You don't have to defend your mother's actions to me, Jennie. I don't know why her going out upset me so much." He sighed and went over to the coffeepot. Pouring himself a cup, he said, "I have to admit I'm jealous of the time she's spending with him." He took a sip and shook his head. "Don't worry, princess. We'll work it out."

Jennie wasn't so sure. Not wanting to dwell on the problem, she fixed herself a cup of peppermint tea and joined her dad at the table. "How's the case going?"

He fixed a blank gaze on her. "What?"

"The investigation—you know, the fire and everything?"

"Hmm. Not great. Too many people with too many opinions and not enough hard evidence. We did find something today, though, that might shed some new light on things."

"What evidence? Can you tell me?"

"Not just now. All I can say is that we've got to be certain of our facts before we make a move. We can't afford any slip-ups. This is a touchy situation from a lot of standpoints."

Jennie wished he would tell her more. At the same time, she wanted to tell him about the list B.J. and Allison had put together. Instead, she shifted directions and asked, "Is Philippe still in jail?"

"For now. He gave us a sworn statement this afternoon, against his lawyer's advice. Says he set the fire because he was angry about the way some of the board members treated him.

He claims he didn't know anyone was in the furnace room." Dad rolled his coffee mug between his hands. "I just wish Carlos would open up. The more I see of that kid, the more I think he knows something."

They sat quietly for a few moments.

"Heard some good news today." Dad set down his cup.

Jennie looked up at him. "What?"

"Come next week, you and Nick will have a school to go to."

"Really? Where?"

"Beaumont offered Trinity the use of an empty warehouse he owns. With a little work, it can be converted into a school. He announced his plans this morning and by noon had enough volunteers and donated materials to get the project done over the weekend."

"Wow. Do you know where it is?"

"Yep. Drove by it this afternoon. It's in Oregon City, just south of the freeway. Not much to look at, but it'll do until they can rebuild."

"That's super. I wonder why Allison and B.J. didn't tell me. I think I'll go call Lisa. She'll be so excited."

"Ah, Jennie." Dad had turned serious again. "Would you mind if I went out for a while?"

"I guess not. Where are you going?"

"I'm not sure. I have some heavy thinking to do."

When the front door closed, Jennie stood there for a moment looking at it, feeling like a part of her had gone with Dad. What would happen next? Her life had been like a roller coaster lately, up one minute, down the next. Now it felt like the train had flown off the tracks. Dad had said not to worry about his relationship with Mom. But how could she not? She couldn't very well turn off her brain.

But you could think about something else, part of her seemed to say. With a deep sigh and a prayer for her parents, Jennie went upstairs to call Lisa. Her room glowed with the rosy light of a sunset. Jennie loved the warm, comfortable feel of it. She sprawled out on her bed, picked up the phone, and dialed.

"Hi, Jen." Lisa greeted. "I was going to call you. I just hung up from talking to Allison, and you'll never guess what she told me."

"You mean about her dad donating the building for the school?"

"How did you know?"

"Dad told me."

"Isn't it cool? My dad's volunteering to help get it ready. I am so excited. Mom says she's proud of how the entire community is coming together to make it happen."

"That is pretty cool," Jennie agreed.

They talked for the next hour about going back to school and how some of the kids had already transferred to other places. Jennie did get some new information. Only the seventh through twelfth graders would be going to the warehouse. The other children would be going to two different churches in the area, both with lots of room that wasn't being utilized during the week. As they talked, Jennie lost some of her earlier enthusiasm. Going to a warehouse in some industrial area had little appeal.

"At least it's a building," Lisa reminded her. "And most of the students will be back together again."

Jennie heard Aunt Kate call Lisa to get off the phone. "Sounds like she's upset about something," Jennie said.

"What else is new? I'm forty-five minutes over my call limit. I'll talk to you tomorrow."

Jennie smiled as she hung up. The one great thing about having her private phone was that she could use it whenever she wanted. The private number had been Mom's idea. Not because Jennie made too many calls, but because so many of the calls coming in were business related. Mom wanted people to get through and felt there would be less friction all around if she gave Jennie her own line.

Jennie had barely hung up when the phone rang again. It was Gavin Winslow.

"Solved the case yet?" Like a lot of sixteen-year-old boys, Gavin's voice cracked as he spoke.

"What makes you think I've been trying to?"

"You telling me you haven't?"

"Not exactly. What about you?"

He chuckled. "That's one of the reasons I called. Wanted to touch base and pool information. I overheard one of the investigative reporters say the police are getting ready to make an arrest. It's all hush-hush. Lots of speculation. Since your dad's on the case, I thought maybe you might know. Truth is, I'd love to beat the other reporters to the punch. The more news stories I can do, the better my chances of being hired after I graduate."

"Sorry, I can't help you. Dad wouldn't tell me anything. They're being careful is all I know."

"Which probably means they're going after somebody big. Like Beaumont."

"You think he started the fire? That's crazy. Mr. Beaumont is letting Trinity use one of his buildings."

"Rent, Jennie. Trinity is renting it with the insurance money they're getting. It's no secret Beaumont has been having financial problems. He recently closed a plant and laid off twenty people."

"That's no reason to torch Trinity."

"Maybe, maybe not. All I know is he'll come out of this deal with a ton of publicity and a lot of cash."

"I can't believe that of Mr. B. Look at all the good he does. He's on the board of directors at church. He sponsored Rafael's entire family and his uncle and Carlos so they can become U.S. citizens." Jennie paced across her rug, remembering what her dad had said about Beaumont believing that Carlos or Philippe might have started the fire.

"Nice guy or not, Jen, he's got motive."

"I suppose." Jennie dropped one knee onto the window seat and peered into the semidarkness. "But he's not the only one." She went on to tell him about Jared and how she'd seen him on the school grounds. "Any one of those people could have set the fire."

"That's true enough. On the other hand, Trinity was well insured. And guess who was on the board when the policies were set up?"

"Beaumont—and Pastor Dave, and Micheal and—"

"Yeah. There are a lot of possibilities, aren't there." His voice shifted up an octave when he said, "Just a minute." When he came back on, he seemed out of breath. "Hey, listen. I gotta go. My ride is here. Call me if you hear anything, okay?"

"Sure." Jennie pressed the disconnect button and sat back on the cushions. She hoped Gavin wasn't getting himself into trouble again. They were alike in a lot of ways. Much to Jennie's chagrin, they had nearly the same bean pole shape. And they both loved investigative work. He wanted to be a reporter; she planned to go to law school.

Jennie leaned forward to watch a brown van turn from Elm onto Magnolia. It slowed down in front of her house. When it passed under the streetlight, she caught a glimpse of the passenger. A young man—maybe still high school age—looked directly at her through an open window, then ducked back inside.

Jennie scooted away from the window, the hairs on the back of her head standing on end. She'd never seen him before, yet he looked familiar. His shaved head reminded her of Jared.

The van passed out of sight. Seconds later Jennie heard the distinct sound of glass breaking.

12

Jennie's heart skidded to a stop. She picked up the phone intent on dialing 9–1–1, then hung up. *Hold on, McGrady. All you heard was breaking glass. That doesn't necessarily equate with burglary.* As for the car, whoever was in it couldn't possibly have stopped and gotten into the house that quickly. Jennie took a deep breath and peeked out her window. Magnolia Drive was quiet as far as she could tell. Part of her wanted to call 9–1–1, stay in her room, and crawl under the bed. Another more curious and adventuresome part wanted to look around. She crept to the door and stepped into the hall, lighted only by a small seashell night-light.

Except for the hum of the refrigerator, the house was quiet. She checked the bathroom and then went across the hall to peek in on Nick and Carlos, thinking one of them may have gotten up and broken a glass or something. The boys were sound asleep.

Of course, it could have been Mom or Dad, she reasoned. Maybe one or both of them had come home while she was on the phone. She moved to her parents' bedroom and pressed her ear against the door. Being slightly ajar, it swung open.

When she didn't find anyone in her parents' bedroom, she sucked in a deep breath and ventured to the stairs. Hugging the wall, Jennie slunk down them, stopping at each step to listen. She'd heard nothing since the breaking glass and was beginning to think she'd imagined the entire thing. From the landing, Jennie scanned the hallway and the dining room and as much of the living room as she could see. No creepy figures pounced out of the shadows. The only movement she could make out was the slight ruffling of the sheer curtain on the dining-room window. Which would have been fine if she'd left the window open. She hadn't.

Jennie hurried down the rest of the steps and flipped on the lights. A cool breeze was coming through a hole the size of a basketball. Glass shards lay on the hardwood floor beneath the window, spreading under the table and chairs.

"The guy in the van must have thrown something in," Jennie mused. It didn't take long to find out what. A grapefruit-sized rock lay on the floor against the dining-room wall. A piece of paper had been rubber banded to it. Jennie started to pick it up, then stopped. There might be prints. Jennie did dial 9–1–1 then.

After explaining what had happened and giving her name and number, Jennie waited. Seeing the flashing lights of a squad car five minutes later, she ran outside to meet them.

"I'm so glad you're here. Someone threw a rock in the window. At first I thought somebody had broken in, but—"

"You're Jennie McGrady?"

Jennie nodded.

"I'm Officer Carey. Can you tell me what happened?"

Jennie explained what she'd seen and heard. By the time she'd finished, another officer arrived. They methodically searched the grounds and house for an intruder before zeroing in on the broken window and the rock.

"What's going on?" Dad stepped into the entry, glancing from one to the other.

Jennie yelped with relief and ran into his arms, nearly knocking him off balance. She related her story again.

"You think it might have been Jared?" Dad asked.

"I don't know. He looked familiar—and the shaved head, but I couldn't be sure."

Dad's gaze swept to the officers. "Have you looked at the note?"

"We were about to." The officers introduced themselves and shook Dad's hand, then knelt to examine the rock.

Using tweezers to protect the integrity of any prints, they carefully opened the note. Officer Carey frowned. "You'd better have a look at this, Lieutenant," he said to Jennie's father.

Dad moved in front of Jennie. Placing a hand on his shoulder, she tried to look between them. Dad stood up, blocking her view.

"Go upstairs, Jennie," Dad ordered, his voice sharp and edged with anger.

"But I want to—"

"Now, Jennie. We'll talk later."

"That's not fair, I—"

"Go!"

Jennie turned abruptly and stomped away. She couldn't remember seeing her father that angry. She hadn't caused it—that much she knew. The anger stemmed from whatever had been written in that note. *Dad is just trying to protect you*, she reasoned. Now she wished she'd picked it up and read it when she'd first seen it. On the other hand, if it was as bad as Dad and Officer Carey seemed to think, her reading it might have been a mistake.

Still, it made her mad. Jennie stood in front of the mirror, examining her cross features. "Scowling doesn't become you," Mom had said on a number of occasions. She was right about that, but at the moment, Jennie didn't care. Pulling her braid forward, she undid it, grabbed a brush, and went to work on the tangles. The sun had bleached her hair in spots, leaving reddish brown highlights. She hadn't noticed that before. But then, she didn't stand in front of the mirror and examine herself all that often either. When she looked up, the frown had disappeared, but the ocean of emotions churning inside hadn't.

After brushing her hair, Jennie grabbed her latest mystery from the dresser and flopped on her bed. Two pages later she set it down. No way could she concentrate on the story when a real live mystery was going on downstairs. Jennie eyed the phone, wishing she could talk to Gram. Not that it would do any good. What could she say? "Gram, you have to do something about your son. Dad is being mean to me. He wouldn't let me see the note some skinhead threw in our living-room window."

Right. Get real, McGrady. Knowing Gram, she'd agree with Dad. But she'd be a whole lot nicer about it. Turning out the light, Jennie moved back over to the bay window and sat down. She imagined the van again, trying to capture any details she might have missed earlier. Had the guy in the van been Jared? She couldn't be sure, but the resemblance was striking. Yet there was something different about him too.

"Maybe it's just wishful thinking." Jennie picked up a stuffed koala bear and hugged it. "Maybe you don't want it to be Jared because that would mean Michael was wrong about him." Jennie wished she could talk to Jared again. Seeing him face-to-face might help.

She needed to talk to Michael again too. It seemed like an eternity since she'd seen him that morning. Since he'd . . . *died.*

A timid knock on her door brought her out of her reverie.

"Come in."

Dad poked his head in. "How come you have the lights out?"

"I was thinking."

"Mind if I turn them on?"

"Go ahead." Jennie would have preferred talking to him

in the dark. She didn't want him seeing her messy room or her.

Nevertheless, the lights came on and Dad came in. He'd taken off his sports jacket and loosened his tie. He looked more relaxed and a lot less angry. "Looks like your room could use some attention."

"I'm behind. Don't worry, I'll get to it." Jennie braced herself for his lecture about watching her tone of voice. The lecture didn't come. Instead, he crossed the room and stood at the window in front of her.

"I'm sorry if I embarrassed you down there, princess. I shouldn't have yelled at you in front of Carey and Sherman."

Jennie shrugged. "I wasn't embarrassed. Just upset. I wanted to see the note. I mean . . . I know you were trying to protect me. Mom would have done the same thing. But how bad can it be?" She shifted over so he could sit beside her.

Dad lowered himself onto the seat, sighed, and hung an arm around her neck. "You don't need to be exposed to language like that. But as offensive as the words were, the worst part of the note was the swastika and the threat."

"So it *was* the skinheads. Did they take responsibility for the fire?"

"No, but that doesn't mean they didn't do it."

"Were they threatening me? Are they mad at me because I turned Jared in when I saw him poking around the fire scene?"

"Not exactly." The expression on Dad's face said it all. It *had* been aimed at her.

She swallowed back a rising tide of panic. "Was it a death threat? I have a right to know."

Dad drew a hand down his face. "I suppose you do." Taking her hand in his, he said, "They've threatened to kill you if I don't release Jared."

13

"The skinheads want you to release Jared?" Jennie finally managed to say. "But you don't have him, do you?"

"No. Like I told you, we questioned him and let him go." The scar on Dad's face twitched as he spoke.

"Well, at least now we know for sure Jared wasn't the guy I saw in the car."

"Not likely. Officer Carey thinks you may have seen his older brother. Carey has dealt with some of these guys before. Rich Reinhardt is the group's leader."

"No wonder Jared has had trouble leaving the group." Jennie jumped up and paced across the floor. "I still don't understand. Why would they think you still had Jared?"

"I have no idea."

"Unless Jared told them that. . . . Dad, suppose Jared is telling the truth and he really does want to leave the gang. He could be hiding somewhere to keep from going back. Maybe he's afraid of what they might do to him."

"Then I guess we'll just have to find him."

Dad stood and stretched. "In the meantime you'd best get ready for bed." He glanced around the room, his expression changing from one of concern to annoyance. "I hope you plan on cleaning this mess up soon."

An all-too-familiar resentment surged through her again. *You have no business criticizing how I keep my room. Mom never did—hardly ever.* Of course, Jennie usually didn't let it get this bad. She clenched her fists and clamped her jaw shut to keep from making the caustic remark. "I'll get to it," she said through clenched teeth.

"Good. It's important to have order in your life, princess. Especially when the world outside is a mess."

Tight-lipped, Jennie nodded. Her anger dissipated some. Dad had a point, but she didn't feel like acknowledging it right now. *You're being defensive, McGrady. Let it go.* Relations between her and her father had been nearly perfect since he'd come home, but in the last few days she'd had feelings of almost wishing he hadn't come back. She didn't want to feel that way.

Jennie shoved the thought aside. "I love you, Dad," she said aloud to reassure herself more than him.

"I love you too, princess." He kissed her cheek and started to leave. At the door he turned back around. "By the way, I stopped by the hospital tonight to see your mother."

"You did?"

"Hmm." The expression on his face indicated the visit hadn't gone well.

Jennie told herself that he might just be tired. "How's Michael?" What she really wanted to ask was: *Did you work everything out? Is everything okay between you two?* But she was afraid to ask that. Afraid the answer might be no.

"No change." Dad hesitated a moment, then said, "I'll be gone by the time you get up in the morning. Have an early breakfast appointment. Your mom said she'd call you around nine."

Jennie nodded and told him about her plan to take Carlos and Nick to Kate's. "Lisa and I have some stuff we need to do."

"Good. Your mother could use the rest." He frowned, looking like he wanted to say more but didn't. "Good night, princess. Sleep tight."

When the door closed, Jennie sank onto her bed. Glancing around her room, she winced at the mess. Dirty clothes lay in heaps where she'd taken them off. Drawers hung halfway open. Her book bag still lay where she'd set it on Monday, unzipped, its contents falling out. Chaos. Just like everything else in her life right now.

Remembering her father's comment about order, she picked up a pair of socks and a shirt that lay at her feet, then scooped up the other clothes littering the floor as she made her way to the closet. She dumped them into the empty laundry basket behind the closet door.

Twenty minutes later the room looked tidy, and Jennie did feel better and a lot more in control. Pajamas on and teeth brushed, Jennie had one more task to do before she could fall asleep. She pulled out the suspect chart she'd started on the fire investigation and added another name: *Rich Reinhardt. Skinhead. Jared's older brother.* Under motive she wrote *revenge.* If Rich knew of Jared's visit to Michael, he could have had more on his mind than prejudice.

Setting the chart aside, she pulled out her diary. She hadn't written in it since the first day of school over a week ago. Reading over the entry brought a smile to her lips.

This is going to be a great year. I'm officially on the swim team. Coach Dayton says I'm the best swimmer she's had in a long time. Jennie stopped reading and leaned back against her pillows remembering. She'd not only made the team, she'd broken a state record.

Friday afternoon after school Jennie had gone to the pool to keep her appointment with Coach Dayton. All the other team members were in place, but because Jennie had been out of town during tryouts the coach wanted her to come in so she could be placed according to her abilities. She'd qualified for nearly everything but the hundred-meter and stood at the ready for the signal to go.

"Come on, Jennie. You can do it!" Lisa yelled from the sidelines.

Bang!

Jennie's lean body sliced into the water and surfaced in the center of the pool. Stroke. Glide. Stroke. Glide. Her long legs kept up a steady rhythm while her arms automatically executed an Australian crawl, her best stroke. While part of her concentrated on staying in her lane and on making turns, another part pretended to be swimming with the dolphins like she had on her vacation with Gram to Florida.

The dolphins were fast and sleek, and when they swam full out, not even the boats could catch them. But for Jennie, they had slowed down as if to give her a fighting chance. Swimming with them had not only made her faster but had more than doubled her endurance. She'd always been a good swimmer; now she was even better.

Jennie came to a stop when her hand raked the side of the pool at the end of her lap. She pulled off her cap and shook her hair free of it.

"Good job, McGrady!" Coach Dayton yelled. She jotted something down on her clipboard. "Keep it up and we'll make state this year. You just beat the hundred-meter record." Diane Dayton, DeeDee for short, gave Jennie a thumbs-up sign. With her trim figure, short hair, and small heart-shaped face, DeeDee looked more like a student than a thirty-five-year-old woman with four kids. "I'm placing you in the hundred-meter freestyle, in the fifty-meter, and in the relay." She grinned and reached down to give Jennie a hand out of the water. "Congratulations, McGrady. Good to have you on the team."

"Thanks." Jennie grabbed a towel. Embarrassed by the accolades from her PE teacher and her cousin and best friend, Lisa, she headed for the showers.

"Come by my office and pick up your schedule," DeeDee shouted. "I want you in here working out with the team every day after school." She ducked into the room near the women's locker room.

Jennie pulled away from the memory. A tear spilled down her cheek. She brushed it away. What would happen to the team now? Had their hopes gone up in smoke too? Jennie hadn't talked to Coach Dayton since the fire. Maybe she'd call tomorrow. Maybe it wasn't too late.

The memory of that Friday afternoon lingered like a familiar tune that wouldn't go away—like something that needed to be repeated. Jennie closed her eyes again and let it play out. "Hey, Jennie!" Gavin Winslow had shouted to her when she'd climbed out of the water that day. "Great finish. I caught it all right here." He held up his camera. "How about one of you standing beside DeeDee."

Jennie swung around. "No more pictures, Gavin."

"C'mon, Jennie, be a sport." Ignoring her protests, he took half a dozen photos. "If you're going to start breaking records, you gotta get used to the publicity."

Jennie made a face at him and walked away. As much as she liked Gavin, she totally disliked being the focus of attention. With all the crimes she'd helped solve lately, Jennie had been in the news more times than the president—well, almost. Gavin was right, she should be getting used to it.

Lisa had stayed in the pool area to talk with Gavin. She shuffled into the locker room as Jennie stepped out of the shower. "Why do you have to be like that?" Lisa asked.

"Like what?"

"You know. Gavin's only doing his job. You were being nasty."

"I know. It's just that I've never liked having my picture taken. I'm too skinny."

"You are not. You're perfect. I'm the one—"

Jennie sighed. "Let's not get into that. Like our moms and Gram are always telling us, we're both just right for who we are."

Lisa grinned. "And don't you forget it. You looked really good out there." She propped a foot on a bench to tie her tennis shoe, her hair shimmering like a new copper penny as it shifted forward. "There is one problem, though. That business with Gavin isn't just because you don't like publicity. You've been acting strange lately. Like you're mad at the world. Mom says it might have something to do with all the adjustments of your mom and dad getting back together."

Jennie frowned. "Having Dad home is definitely not a problem."

"Okay, I didn't say it was. I'm just saying that for five years it was just you, your mom, and Nick. It can't be easy having another parent living with you."

"I like having Dad there. He belongs with us."

"Of course he does. . . ." Lisa glanced at her watch. "Never mind. We need to get going. I told Allison and B.J. we'd be there at five. It's almost that now."

Jennie finished toweling off and pulled on her blue cotton shorts and tank top. While slipping her bare feet into a pair of white sandals, she pulled her wet hair into a ponytail, then grabbed her book bag.

A strong smell accosted them when they reached the hall. "What's that smell?"

Lisa shrugged. "I don't . . ."

Goose bumps broke out on Jennie's bare arms. "Smoke." She sniffed again.

"Maybe it's that old furnace." Lisa wrinkled her nose. "The new janitor still hasn't gotten the hang of it."

"Maybe." Jennie stopped at the coach's office to get the schedule. "We'd better check it out."

DeeDee smelled the smoke too. "It's probably nothing or the fire alarm would have gone off by now." Her concerned gaze caught Jennie's. "Still, we should report it. Better to be safe than sorry." She picked up the phone, punched the numbers to the school office, and reported the smoke. After listening for a few seconds, she cradled the phone. "Just as I thought. Nothing serious. Philippe is working on the furnace. Sure will be glad when we get a new one. The money has been set aside. Just has to be okayed by the board."

Jennie opened her eyes, turning off the memory. That had been on a Friday. The fire had started on Monday. The faint smell of smoke lingered in her mind. The alarm hadn't gone off then. Why? Had Philippe turned it off while he was working on the furnace?

The possibility played in Jennie's mind. What if Philippe had turned off the alarm when it was smoking so it wouldn't keep going off? What if he'd forgotten to turn it back on? That meant it could have been an accident all along. Maybe Carlos had been playing with matches and accidentally set the fire.

"That would explain his silence." Jennie bounced out of bed and headed downstairs to talk to Dad. She stopped at the landing. All the lights were out, which meant he'd probably gone to bed. She retreated back to the hall and started to knock on her parents' bedroom door when she heard her father snoring.

Sighing, she went back to her room. Tomorrow would be soon enough to tell him about the fire alarm. Turning off the overhead light, Jennie used the illuminated numbers on her clock radio to direct her steps to the bed. Twelve-thirty. She crawled into bed and switched on her bedside lamp, then set the alarm for five A.M. That should get her up early enough to catch Dad before he left.

Jennie turned off her lamp and snuggled under the covers. True to form, while her body was more than ready to go to sleep, her mind refused to shut down. It raced with possibilities and questions. Who had set the fire? Had it been an accident? Where was Dad going so early in the morning, and who did he have an appointment with?

Jennie punched her pillow and squeezed her eyes closed, willing herself to go to sleep.

14

The alarm went off at five. Jennie eyed the glaring red numbers, groaned in dismay, and turned it off. She'd managed to fall asleep sometime after one and was definitely not in the mood to get up yet. She did need to talk to Dad before he left. Promising herself she'd lie there just another couple of minutes, Jennie yawned and stretched, then closed her eyes.

"Watch this." Nick giggled.

The mattress shifted as he climbed onto it. Barely aware of his presence, Jennie rolled over onto her stomach. "Go 'way, Nick."

"She always does that." Nick giggled. "Sometimes I play horsey on her back, but sometimes I just tickle her."

Jennie rubbed her eyes. "Who are you talking to?"

"Carlos."

Jennie bolted upright. "Oh." She glanced at the clock and moaned. "It's after eight already. Why didn't you wake me up sooner?" Her gaze flitted between the two boys. They were both dressed, and from the stains on Nick's turquoise shirt, they'd already eaten.

"Me and Carlos was watching telebision. He made me breakfast and everything."

"I see that." Jennie tossed Carlos a smile. "Thanks for taking care of him for me."

Carlos's gaze swept to the floor. He still wasn't talking.

"You guys better scoot so I can get dressed." She waved them away.

"You promised we could go play with Kurt. We're still going, right?"

"I think so."

Nick turned to Carlos. "Kurt gots the neatest tree fort. We play jungle and G.I. Joes and lots of stuff."

When they'd gone, Jennie threw her covers aside and made her way to the bathroom. A hot shower, though quicker than usual, revived her, bringing back all the questions she'd gone to sleep with, including the one about who Dad was having breakfast with.

Frustrated with herself for sleeping in, Jennie stood in front of her closet looking for something suitable to wear. Nearly everything she had was in the laundry basket. She definitely needed to wash clothes. With no clean jeans or shorts, Jennie settled on a pink cotton sundress and sandals. She rarely wore dresses, but since she'd be interviewing people, Jennie figured the dress wouldn't hurt.

Mom called at eight-forty-five as Jennie was stuffing a load of white clothes into the washer.

"How's everything there? Are Carlos and Nick getting along?"

"Fine and yes. What's going on with Michael?" Jennie scooped up a measure of soap, poured it over the clothes, and turned the machine on while Mom filled her in.

"He's still on life support. Pastor Dave and Maddie Winslow volunteered to sit with him today. I don't know what happened to Reverend Cole. Anyway, I should be home by nine-thirty."

"We'll be gone by then." Jennie explained her plans to leave Carlos and Nick with Aunt Kate while she and Lisa helped Allison and B.J. with a project.

"This project wouldn't have anything to do with the fire, would it?"

"I doubt it," Jennie said. "Allison and B.J. think maybe one of the people Mr. Beaumont had to lay off might have started it for revenge, but it doesn't seem very logical to me."

"Did you talk to your father about it? Sounds like something he would want to know."

"Not yet, but I plan to. And don't worry. We're going in pairs."

"All right, I suppose it won't hurt. But, Jennie, don't be gone too long. I hate imposing on Kate."

If you stayed home more, maybe we wouldn't have to, Jennie felt like saying, but didn't. "Kate said it wouldn't be any trouble. You know how she likes having other kids around to play with Kurt."

"I know. Plan on being home by four so you can fix dinner."

Jennie agreed and hung up, feeling annoyed and resentful again. It wasn't fair that Mom was gone so much. *Michael's injuries aren't fair either,* she reminded herself. *And Mom's right. Someone should be there for him.* Jennie just wished it didn't have to be her mother.

Lisa and Jennie met Allison and B.J. at twelve-thirty at Better Times, a book, gift, and coffee shop in Lake Oswego. Allison had suggested the meeting to talk about how their morning of interviewing had gone.

"Did you find anybody suspicious on your list?" Allison peered over the menu.

"No one." Jennie handed her list of names to Allison. "Dead ends."

"Not for us." B.J. pulled a scrunched-up paper out of her back pocket. "Al and I think we may have a couple leads."

She unfolded the paper and pressed out the creases. "This guy—Gary Stanford—is our best bet. He's an engineer. When we went to his house he was gone, but four of the people we talked to said he'd threatened to *do something* to Dad. One lady said he still wasn't working and that he was staying home with his three kids and not having an easy time of it."

"Okay," Jennie said. "I'll have Dad check him out. You said you had a couple of guys. Who's the other one?"

"Fred Desmond. He was close to retirement and hasn't been able to find a job. And get this—he filed a lawsuit against Dad for age discrimination."

Jennie jotted both names and addresses down.

"I still don't think you should tell your dad yet," B.J. said. "At least not until we've checked them out for ourselves."

"I don't think that's such a good idea. If one of them really did do it—"

"Please, Jennie." Allison wiped her mouth with her napkin. "Dad will be furious if he finds out we turned these guys over to the police without good cause. He made it very clear he didn't want his employees hassled."

"Maybe we could all four go together," B.J. suggested.

Jennie looked at each of them. "I think we'd be too intimidating, but we could all go and two of us could wait in the car while the other two go in. That way if there's trouble, the other two could go for help."

"And," Lisa added, "there's less chance of trouble when the person knows we're in a group."

"Perfect." B.J. crunched a potato chip for emphasis. "We'll go right after lunch."

Growing curiosity made Jennie volunteer to go in with B.J. to visit both suspects. Curiosity plus the fact that Lisa and Allison had both turned chicken. Fred Desmond was first on the list. His wife, a white-haired woman who walked with a cane, answered the door, greeting them with a hesitant smile.

"Hi," B.J. introduced herself, then Jennie. "Is your husband in?"

"N-no, I'm . . . afraid . . . not." Mrs. Desmond spoke haltingly. Her head wobbled when she talked, like Grandpa Calhoun, and Jennie guessed she had Parkinson's Disease.

"Could we come in and talk with you for a few minutes, then?" Jennie asked.

"Certainly. Where . . . are my manners?" She led them inside, asked them to make themselves comfortable, and set a plate of cookies on the coffee table before cautiously lowering her small frame into a chair. "Did you say your name was Beau . . . mont? You wouldn't be our Mr. Beaumont's . . . daughter, would you?"

"Yes. I'm really sorry about your husband losing his job." B.J. reached for a cookie. "My father is very concerned about everyone he had to lay off."

"Is he?" She fingered a delicate crocheted doily similar to the kind Grandma Calhoun used to make. "That's very nice of him."

"Yes. Um—has your husband been able to find a job yet?"

"No. But . . . I wouldn't . . . worry about it, dear. He's . . . suing . . . the pants off your father."

"I heard about that," B.J. said. "Dad didn't want to close the plant or lay people off. He couldn't afford to keep it going."

"Oh, I know that, dear. We harbor . . . no hard feelings. It's . . . the only option open at the moment."

"M-maybe I could talk to Dad about hiring your husband in another facility."

"That's not . . . likely. Fred will be able to retire . . . in another year. All we want . . . are the benefits he has coming to him."

Jennie tuned them out and nibbled at a peanut butter

cookie while she glanced around the modest house. Family photos and knickknacks covered nearly every available space. She picked up a gold-rimmed plate and smiled as she read the inscription. The date, written under a pair of wedding bells, read *Married September 8, 1957*. The fire had been set on the eighth.

"I see you just celebrated your fortieth anniversary." Jennie showed the plate to B.J.

"Yes." A radiant smile transformed Mrs. Desmond's lined face. "Our son . . . William . . . lives in Pasadena—he's a lawyer, you know. He flew us down there for a big family reunion. We . . . just got back into town yesterday."

Jennie nodded. "Is he handling the lawsuit?"

"Why, yes, how did you know?"

"Just a wild guess." Jennie started for the door. "We'd better go, B.J." Turning back, they thanked Mrs. Desmond and wished her and her husband well.

"Don't tell Dad I said this," B.J. said as they walked out to the car, "but I hope they win the lawsuit."

Jennie grinned. "Me too."

"I don't understand why Dad let him go like that. Maybe I should talk to him. I'll bet he would hire him back."

"I wouldn't count on it, B.J. I've heard about companies downsizing, and they do whatever they need to save money."

"Dad's not like that. My father probably doesn't know about Fred. Dad has a lot of people working for him. Not everything gets his attention."

The next suspect, Gary Stanford, greeted them at the door wearing a perplexed look on his face and diaper over his shoulder. "Who did you say you were with?" he asked when B.J. introduced herself.

"We're not with anyone—not exactly. My father—David Beaumont—is very concerned about all the people he had to lay off and . . . well, we're just wondering how you're doing. I guess you must be pretty upset."

A baby started crying in the background. He looked inside, then back at B.J. and Jennie. "Um—I'm kind of busy right now. Um—" A loud crash and a scream interrupted him.

Gary left them standing at the door and raced inside. Jennie hesitated only a second before following him in. He stood transfixed as if he didn't know what to do next. The living room was in a shambles. One baby sat on the floor chewing on a plastic ring. A girl about four stood next to a counter that separated the living room and kitchen. She looked ready to cry. "I didn't mean to, Daddy."

Jennie followed the little girl's teary gaze to the tipped-over end table and the shattered glass vase beside it. She spotted the child's head behind the table just as he began wailing.

She and Gary headed for him at the same time. Gary ran both hands through his hair. "Oh my . . . Tiffany, what have you done?"

"I didn't, Daddy. Brian just falleded."

Brian lay on his back, screaming and gagging, his mouth full of blood. Jennie scooped up the child and held him so the blood could drain forward. Without asking, she grabbed the diaper Gary had over his shoulder and dabbed at the wound in Brian's lower lip.

Gary still had that vacant look. "I—we better get him to the hospital."

"It probably isn't as bad as it looks," Jennie yelled over the wailing. All three of the children were crying now. "He must have hit his mouth on the table and bit through his lip. My little brother did that once. Could you get me a cold washcloth?"

Seconds later he came back with one, and Jennie washed off the blood around the mouth, touching the bloody lip tenderly. Brian caught the wet cloth in his mouth and began sucking on it. Little by little the wailing turned to whimpers. B.J. had picked up and comforted the other baby, while Gary held Tiffany. "It's okay, honey," he told her. "It was an accident."

His gaze shifted to Jennie. "Is he going to be okay?"

Jennie removed the cloth and examined the split lip. "I think so. You might want to take him to the emergency room. Sometimes they do stitches. Nick—that's my brother—didn't need them, but it's hard to tell."

"Look, um . . . what was your name again?"

Jennie told him and reintroduced B.J.

"I don't know how to thank you. I'm kind of new at this."

"No problem." After looking at the cut in Brian's lip again, Jennie suggested she go with Gary to the hospital while the others stay with the two uninjured children and clean up the mess.

"Whatever you say, Jennie." Gary reached into his pocket, extracting a set of keys. "You seem to have things well in hand."

Jennie talked to Allison, B.J., and Lisa about her plan. They were more than willing to help and were already cleaning the living room when Jennie and Gary left.

Gary drove his Lexus while Jennie held little Brian on her lap. He was nearly sleeping and had snuggled comfortably against her. "He's so cute." Jennie tenderly brushed a lock of damp blond hair from his forehead. "Are he and Brandy twins? They look so close to the same age."

He nodded. "That was a surprise. We'd only planned on having two kids . . . but life doesn't always follow our plans."

Jennie chuckled. "That's for sure. My friends and I were only going to talk with you for five minutes, maybe ten. And here I am, riding with you to the hospital. Strange."

"Right. What was it you wanted to talk to me about?"

Jennie felt certain Gary was not the type of person to resort to arson but decided to question him anyway—especially now that she had the opportunity. "We've been questioning the people Mr. Beaumont laid off to see how they're getting along."

"Why would you do that?"

"Mr. Beaumont is concerned about you. And—" Jennie glanced over at him and down at the baby in her arms and opted to come right out and ask. "We're questioning everyone connected with the layoffs to see if anyone is carrying a grudge. There's a possibility one of the people who worked for him set fire to our church to get even."

He frowned and shook his head. "I can't imagine any of us doing something like that."

"Several employees said you had threatened to *do something*."

"Oh yeah." Tipping his head to the side, he added, "I'll have to admit I was pretty riled at first. I won't honestly say I didn't plot revenge. I must have put in a hundred job applications. My wife went out and got a great job producing a couple of news shows for a television studio, and well, rather than hire a sitter, I took over her responsibilities at home." He grinned at her. "As you can see I'm still a bit green, but I kind of like it."

"So you aren't still mad at Mr. Beaumont?"

"No. Beaumont was doing what he had to do. Looking back, I guess I'd have to be thankful if anything. I've gotten closer to my kids than I ever would have otherwise."

Gary pulled up to the emergency entrance. "How about you park this thing while I take Brian in?"

Jennie agreed, parked the car, and was walking back to the building when she saw a familiar figure making his way through the parking lot.

"Dad! Hey, wait up."

"Hi." He greeted her with a customary hug. "What brings you down here? Where are Nick and Carlos?"

Jennie briefly explained as they walked toward the hospital entrance.

"I thought I asked you to watch Carlos. I need to know when and if he decides to talk."

"I know. And from now on I will. But I promised B.J. and Allison I'd interview their dad's ex-employees."

"You should have come to me."

Jennie explained that too. "It turned out to be a dead end. Look at it this way, we saved the police department a lot of legwork."

He stopped before ascending the steps leading into the hospital and shook his head. "I don't know what I'm going to do with you, princess." With a sigh he added, "None of that matters much now anyway. I think we've found the arsonist."

"Really? Who?"

"Don't let this get out. We won't be announcing it to the press until after we make a formal arrest, which should be sometime this afternoon."

"I won't say anything to anyone, Dad. I promise. Who is it?"

"Marissa Cole."

15

"You're kidding, right?" Jennie gave her father an incredulous look. But he wasn't kidding. Dad wouldn't joke about something like that. "Reverend Cole?"

"We found evidence at the scene and in her apartment. She was in the building when the fire broke out."

"Sure. At the board meeting."

"No. In putting the pieces together, we discovered that the fire had been set just before the meeting. The board members were just coming in." Putting a hand at Jennie's back, he nudged her toward the sliding-glass doors.

"So it could have been any of the board members."

"It could, but the evidence leads to Reverend Cole."

"Is she here? Did you come to arrest her?"

"No. I came down to tell your mother. Didn't want her finding out on the news or some other way."

"Good idea, but I thought Mom was home."

"She was for about three hours." Dad punched the up button on the elevator with a little more vigor than necessary.

"Why did she come back? I thought someone was relieving her this afternoon."

"Apparently no one else is as committed to this as your mother."

"Dad . . ."

"You don't need to explain. Your mother is doing what

she feels she needs to do. Can't argue with that. Humph. I feel bad even complaining about it."

The elevator doors swished open and Dad mumbled, "I'll talk to you later."

Jennie caught her father's arm. "Are you sure it was Marissa? What about the threatening notes she got?"

"That was the clincher for me, princess. Marissa sent those notes to herself."

"But, Dad—" Jennie started to dispute the allegation. None of it made sense. Reverend Cole was a wonderful, giving person.

"I know you have a lot of questions. So do I, but this isn't the time or place to discuss it. We'll talk later—at home."

They parted then, Jennie veering toward the emergency room and Dad taking the elevator up to the burn unit. At the emergency room, she caught up with Gary, who was trying to fill out some forms and hold the squirming Brian at the same time.

"Can I help?" Jennie extended her arms to Brian, who seemed more than willing to escape his father's grasp.

"Thanks. I never noticed before how many hands you need to be a parent." Gary tossed her a wry grin. "I tell you, I have a great deal of respect for moms these days."

While Gary filled out the papers, Jennie took Brian to a corner of the room loosely termed the children's play area. While part of her mind focused on watching Brian, another part drifted back to the day of the fire. The waiting room had been full then. Mrs. Beaumont and Mom were waiting to hear about Mr. Beaumont and Michael. Mr. Talbot had been there too.

Poor Mrs. Talbot. Jennie frowned. In all the worry over Michael and the business with her parents, she had forgotten about the school secretary.

"Brian Stanford?" A nurse stood at the emergency room door, a clip chart in her hand.

Gary, who'd finished his forms, snatched up his son. "Want to come in with us, Jennie?"

"Sure." Jennie made a mental note to check on Mrs. Talbot and pay her a visit soon.

"Watch this, Jennie!" Nick shouted as he stood at the side of the Beaumonts' pool and waved his skinny little arms. "I'm gonna jump in."

"I'm watching." She stretched out on the chaise lounge and sipped on a tall glass of pink lemonade. After such a hectic afternoon it felt good to vegetate and unwind. Upon leaving the Stanfords' home, Allison and B.J. had invited Jennie, Lisa, their brothers, and Carlos over to swim. Jennie hadn't hesitated to accept. She'd called home from Lisa's and left a message on the machine, borrowed a swimsuit from Aunt Kate, and here she was. Lisa was lying on a chaise lounge beside her, and Allison and B.J. were inside fixing a snack.

Brian hadn't needed stitches after all, and Jennie felt relieved that Gary was not the arsonist. All four of the girls agreed that he was much too busy playing Mr. Mom to be considered a suspect.

Jennie didn't believe Reverend Cole was the arsonist either. Yet Dad seemed so certain. And they had evidence. Motive, means, and opportunity. Jennie could hardly wait to talk with her father. She also wished she could tell her friends.

"Come on, Nick. I'll catch you." Kurt stood chest high in the turquoise water, reaching for his younger cousin.

Carlos sat on a step at the shallow end, moving his hands back and forth and staring at the rippling water as though it held a secret.

"He looks so sad," Lisa murmured. "I wish there was something we could do."

"Maybe bringing him here wasn't the best idea." Jennie set her drink down. "It probably reminds him of his dad."

Jennie itched to tell him his dad would be released soon now that the police had another suspect. But that would have to wait until the police made Reverend Cole's arrest public.

"I wonder what he saw that upset him so much." Lisa lifted a hand to shade her eyes from the late afternoon sun.

"Me too."

"Hey, great news!" Allison emerged from the house carrying a tray heaped with fruits and veggies.

"They made an arrest in the arson case and released Philippe?" Jennie piped up.

"No." Allison gave her a have-you-lost-your-mind look. "Dad just called to say they got most of the inside walls framed today at our temporary school. They'll do the wiring and Sheetrock tomorrow. He's really pleased about the progress."

"That's great." Lisa snagged a carrot stick from the tray when Allison set it down.

B.J. set down a plate of assorted cookies. "Aren't you going to tell them the best part?"

Allison raised her eyes. "You mean the gym?"

"That and the pool. It's almost ready."

"Great!" Jennie felt a ton lighter than she had all week.

"Dad just talked to Coach Dayton," B.J. continued, "and she wants us there tonight to finish cleaning the place up, then we'll practice."

"Tonight?" Jennie glanced over at the boys. Nick and Kurt had coaxed Carlos into the water and the three were playing catch. "You going?"

"Of course." B.J. sank into one of the white metal chairs at the glass-topped table and bit into a chocolate chip cookie. "Aren't you?"

Jennie shrugged. Much as she wanted to, with Mom gone there'd be dinner and dishes, not to mention watching the boys. She related those things and added, "I was planning to visit Michael and Mrs. Talbot tonight too. What time does DeeDee want us there?"

"Six-thirty. I was hoping you'd pick me up. I could get a ride, but I'd rather go with you."

"I'll have to check with my parents." The sound of laughter dragged Jennie's attention back to the pool. "Did you hear that?" Jennie whispered, not wanting Carlos to hear. "He's laughing."

Kurt had the ball balanced on his nose. Nick and Carlos were trying to knock it off. "My turn, my turn." Carlos grabbed the ball and set it on his nose.

When Jennie arrived home at five-thirty, Mom was there fixing a salad. The kitchen smelled lived-in and warm. The bread machine beeped three times, letting them know the baking cycle had finished.

Mom hugged Jennie, then Nick and Carlos, and sent the boys out to feed and water Bernie. "He missed you today, Nick. Why don't you take the ball out and play catch."

"Come on, Carlos." Nick took the older boy's hand. "I'll let you put the food in Bernie's dish."

Carlos had retreated again but seemed to like the idea of playing with Bernie.

"I didn't think you'd be home yet." Jennie peeked into the oven. Hot air perfumed with garlic, Worcestershire sauce, and whatever other spices Mom had used on the baking chicken warmed her face. For a moment life seemed almost normal again.

"Maddie offered to relieve me. I thought you might like to help work on the pool."

"I do." Jennie retrieved an apple from the freshly filled fruit basket. "Thanks."

Mom smiled. "So how was your day? Did you get to talk to all the people you wanted to?"

Jennie crunched down on the apple and nodded. "Yep. We could have saved ourselves the trouble." She told Mom about the interviews and her trip to the hospital. "Dad tell you about Reverend Cole?"

Mom gave Jennie an odd look, snapped off a piece of plastic wrap, and covered the salad bowl. "He did." She set the bowl in the fridge and shut the door harder than necessary.

"I take it you don't agree."

Mom's gaze met hers. "You have to ask?"

"Guess not. Did Dad tell you what evidence they had?"

"Not specifically." Mom opened the oven and turned over the sizzling pieces of chicken. "I don't care what your father or the DA or anyone else says, Marissa Cole is not an arsonist."

"You think someone set her up?"

"What other explanation is there?" Mom backed away from the stove, her face red from the heat.

Jennie didn't have an answer but she knew someone who might. "Carlos talked today."

Mom poured herself a cup of coffee. "Really?"

"He didn't say much, but it's a start."

"Why don't you come sit with me at the table and tell me about it."

Jennie straddled the chair, much as one would a horse, and complied. It felt better than good having Mom back home. When she finished telling her about Carlos, Jennie sighed and slouched in the chair. "I haven't asked him about the fire yet. Guess I'm afraid he'll stop talking again."

"It's best not to move too fast. He needs to feel comfortable with us and trust us. Maybe we shouldn't talk to him about it at all. From what I know about these things, it's best to wait until he decides to open up on his own."

The comfortable mood remained all through dinner.

Carlos and Nick giggled like old friends. Dad seemed in a better mood than he had all week. Mom was even looking healthier. Things were definitely looking up. Except for Reverend Cole. Dad hadn't brought the subject up—probably to keep from upsetting Carlos—but while she was getting ready to leave for the pool clean-up party, Jennie caught the story on television.

"The investigation into Monday's arson fire at a local church and school took a bizarre twist today when police arrested Reverend Marissa Cole late this afternoon. The DA's office says they have strong evidence to support the case against the former missionary. Reverend Cole will be arraigned tomorrow morning at nine-thirty. Cole had little to say to reporters this evening. Friends and relatives are shocked. We'll keep you updated on this story as it unfolds."

"Better hurry, Jennie," Mom called from the dining room, where she was washing off the table. "You'll be late."

"But this is important." She sighed.

"We'll fill you in when you get home," Dad said.

Jennie kissed him on the cheek. "See you."

She gave her mother a long hug. "Thanks, Mom."

Tears filled her mother's eyes, but she was smiling. "Scoot."

Outside, Jennie stopped briefly to say good-bye to Nick and Carlos.

"Where you going?" Nick asked.

"To the school. I'm going to help clean up. . . ." Jennie's voice faded as she watched Carlos's expression change from innocent curiosity to fear. "What's wrong, Carlos?"

He wrapped his arms around Bernie's neck. Silent again.

16

"Dad wasn't kidding when he said they'd gotten a lot done." B.J. leaned out the car window. "It hardly looks like there's even been a fire."

"I guess it shows you what people can do when they work together." The first thing Jennie noticed from the top of the hill above the school was the roof on the gym. Workers had cleaned and restored it to its peacock brilliance. Much of the debris from the fire had been removed. The heavy equipment made the grounds look like a building site rather than a crime scene. The only obvious evidence of the fire was a cavernous black concrete hole in the ground that had once been the basement and furnace room. Yellow tape still surrounded the perimeters of the burned-out building, and signs warned people to stay out.

A sign also directed Jennie to drive around to the parking lot on the far side of the gym.

"Looks like a lot of people turned out." Jennie pulled into an empty spot.

"Which means we'll get done faster. Hey, look. There's Gavin." B.J. waved and climbed out of the car. "Hey, Gav. How's it going?"

"It's about time you two got here." Gavin chucked a piece of debris he'd picked up from the still-blackened grass into a dumpster and brushed off his gloved hands.

"We're not that late." Jennie glanced around at the dozens of people busy with various tasks. "What are we supposed to do?"

"DeeDee's got a work detail all mapped out. I think you're assigned to the locker rooms."

Gavin's gaze fell on B.J. "You bring your camera?"

"No. What do I need it here for?"

"This is news. I want us to run a series of articles on the fire and the clean-up efforts. You were supposed to write this one, remember?"

B.J. shrugged. "I'll write it. Just didn't know you wanted pictures."

"If you're going to be a journalist, you always want to think photos." He pushed his glasses back against the bridge of his nose. "Never mind. I'll get some shots today, but you need to get into the habit of carrying your camera around. You never know when a great photo opportunity will come up."

Bewildered, Jennie looked from one to the other. "I didn't know you were interested in journalism, B.J."

"Gavin needed an assistant on the school paper and yearbook, so I volunteered. Thought it might be fun."

"You're still planning on doing a newspaper?" Jennie asked. "I mean, didn't we lose all the equipment?"

"It's been replaced." Gavin's eyes shone brighter than headlights on high beam. "*The Oregonian* went together with some of the other local publishers and raised the money for our journalism and English department."

"Oh, that reminds me," B.J. said. "Dad said someone is donating sixty computers to the school and giving us free online access for a year."

"Who is it? Maybe I can still get the story into *The Oregonian* tonight." He checked his watch. "I can call it in."

"I don't know. He said the donor wanted to remain anonymous."

"Well, tell me what you've got and I'll call it in to the paper. It'll run tomorrow." After getting the details from B.J., he loped off to the pay phone at the gym's entrance.

Jennie and B.J. went in search of Coach Dayton and found her testing the water in the newly filled pool.

"Jennie, B.J." DeeDee rose and greeted each of them with an exuberant hug. "Glad you could make it."

"Where do you want us?"

Putting an arm around them both, she ushered them into the locker room. "In here. The locker rooms weren't damaged by the fire, but everything is covered with soot." Picking up two trays, she handed them each one. "You'll find rags, gloves, and a cleaning solution in these. We already used a power washer to get most of the dirt off, but everything needs to be gone over with cleaner and dried. There are some step stools you can use to reach the top of the lockers. Just wash everything down."

"Hi, guys," Tracy, one of the girls on the swim team, emerged from a shower stall.

The tall, athletic Courtney Evans, Gavin's girlfriend—who used to color her hair a different color every week but now had a natural-looking ash brown shag—peeked around one of the locker rows at them. "About time you got here."

Each of the girls had been assigned a section, and Jennie set to work on hers. She was to do row three of the lockers and the two benches in front of them. The locker room wasn't very big, and within an hour the four girls had finished it.

DeeDee did a quick inspection. "Good work, girls. Go ahead and suit up. It's seven-thirty already. Better hustle."

Jennie shrugged into her swimsuit, still self-conscious about the public changing area and showers that afforded no privacy whatsoever. Maybe if she'd had a figure like most of the other girls, it wouldn't have been so bad. But Jennie had about as many curves as a telephone pole. That was a

McGrady trait, which Gram and Aunt Kate bore witness to. Jennie adjusted the straps of her royal blue one-piece suit and joined the others on the bleachers, where Gavin sat with his camera.

DeeDee outlined her expectations for swim team members, of which there were twelve. Six girls and six boys. One of the guys, Russ Brown, sidled up to Jennie and in a deep whisper said, "Good to have you on the team, Jennie." Russ, a senior, was the team's star diver. More than once Jennie had admired his form as he'd executed his dives in competition. Her stomach fluttered at his open admiration.

"Thanks." Jennie returned his smile. Russ had been part of Trinity since Jennie could remember. His dad was a board member. Jennie automatically added his name to her suspect list. She really should have a talk with all the board members. Since any one of them could have started the fire prior to the meeting, they were all suspect—especially those who weren't hurt. It stood to reason that if they knew what was coming, they'd be able to get out right away.

"Was your dad hurt in the fire?" Jennie asked.

Russ shook his head. "He was late, and by the time he got here the fire was going full blast. Dad's the one who called the fire in on his cell phone."

Jennie nodded and tried to concentrate on her coach. Her mind had ideas of its own. The biggest problem Jennie had with any of the board members was motive. Why would they burn down their church and the place where their kids went to school? It didn't make sense. *And why are you even thinking about it, McGrady? The case is closed. Reverend Cole did it.*

"No," Jennie mumbled. "She couldn't have."

"What did you say?" Russ asked, his voice low and rumbly. B.J. looked up at Jennie with the same question in her eyes.

"N-nothing," Jennie whispered, then turned her attention back to DeeDee.

"I expect you all to be here every day after school and on Saturday mornings. We've got a lot of talent and I can see us going to state."

Several of the team members cheered. Gavin snapped a few photos. Russ whistled in agreement and nudged Jennie.

DeeDee waited for the group to quiet down. "That means daily practice, along with weight lifting, stretching, and endurance swimming." DeeDee went on to give them their placements on the team. Jennie felt tired just listening to the requirements. Swim team would definitely take a huge chunk out of her day. She wondered briefly when she'd have time to work on the case. *You don't have to, McGrady*, an inner voice reminded her. *The case has already been solved.*

A movement by the men's locker room caught her eye. When she looked again, whoever had been there was gone. Jennie rubbed her arms to ward off a sudden chill. *The room is cold, that's all*, she told herself.

"McGrady." DeeDee's stern voice dragged Jennie's mind back to where it belonged. "I don't know what you think you're going to see coming out of the men's room, but I'd appreciate it if you could stay focused on what I'm saying."

B.J. elbowed her and snickered. Jennie started to defend herself, then stopped. It wouldn't help, and DeeDee had already gone on with her instructions. Still, an embarrassed flush warmed her cheeks. She fixed her gaze on DeeDee's clipboard and tried harder to concentrate on what the coach was saying.

"As you know, we lost a couple of students who'd planned to be on the team with us. Shawn Masters and Kelly Dupont transferred out. But we're going to do just fine. We have three newcomers this fall—Jennie McGrady, Katy Anderson, and B.J. Beaumont. I've seen what these girls can do and believe me, we're in for a fantastic year." She paused and encouraged the rest of the team members to give them assistance, encouragement, and to help them adjust to the routine. "Since we don't have a lot of time tonight, I thought we'd have some fun. I've separated you into four relay teams—three members each."

The coach teamed Jennie up with Brian, a junior, and B.J. Brian swam first, then B.J. At the end of the second leg, their team trailed Russ's by nearly half a lap. Russ dove into the water. Jennie followed on his heels. She'd swim hard to catch up, stay even until the last lap, then go all out. Russ had issued a challenge she couldn't ignore. Just prior to the gun, Jennie had overheard him tell his teammates they'd win, no sweat. Well, they might win, but she had no intention of making it easy for him.

While Jennie swam with her imaginary dolphins, she thought about how ordinary things seemed again. Only a couple of days ago the school had been in ruins. Now they had their pool and gymnasium back. And come Monday they'd be back in school. Everything was coming together. She remembered a poster she'd seen somewhere of wild flowers growing among the charred remains of a forest fire. Beneath the photo was part of a Bible verse from Isaiah 61: *The Lord gives . . . beauty for ashes.*

"Come on, Jennie. Go, go, go!" she could hear the other two members of her relay team yell. From the sound of it, they were all cheering for her.

Jennie hit the wall, ending her fourth and final lap. She'd had to work hard to keep up with Russ.

"It's a tie!" DeeDee announced.

Russ leaned on the blue nylon rope that separated the lanes. "Good job, Jennie."

"Thanks." She pulled off her cap, letting her hair cascade into the water, then tipped her head back to wet it and slick it back from her face.

Russ leaned closer, his eyes turning serious. "Um . . . you want to go somewhere after practice?"

"Can't. I have to take B.J. home."

"Tomorrow?"

Jennie shrugged. "Maybe. Give me a call."

Russ pulled himself out of the pool and reached a hand down to Jennie. His blue-gray eyes reminded her of Ryan's, but the resemblance stopped there.

Ryan was blond; Russ had rich chestnut brown hair. Ryan was thinner and an inch or two taller. Russ had the powerful shoulders of a swimmer. Annoyed by the direction her thoughts had taken, Jennie squeezed the water from her hair and grabbed a towel.

"That's it, kids," DeeDee said. "Official practice starts Monday. I'll be here all day tomorrow and strongly urge you to come by. Thanks for all your help in getting things ready. God is turning our ashes into roses."

"How do you do it, McGrady?" B.J. asked as they settled in her car a few minutes later.

"Do what?"

"You attract guys like flies."

"Oh, come on, B.J. You're exaggerating."

"Am not. Russ likes you."

"You think so?" Jennie stuck the key in the ignition and started the car.

"Yeah."

"You're not jealous, are you?"

"No way." B.J. flipped a hand through her curls. "I think it's cool. Russ is a great guy."

"He is nice." Jennie's grin faded. "Too bad. I'm not interested. In case you've forgotten, I already have a boyfriend. Besides, I have more important things to think about than guys."

"Like finding out who really started the fire?"

"What are you, a mind reader?"

"No, I just feel the same way. I don't think Reverend Cole set that fire. Not in a million years."

"Do you have any idea who did?"

B.J. sighed. "Not a clue. I mean, it would be really easy to say Jared did it, or Carlos, or Philippe. There are just too many suspects."

"For sure. Makes me wonder why I'm even worrying about it. Part of the time I'm thinking let the police take care of it. And part of the time I'm trying to come up with the answer."

"Yeah. I know what you mean." B.J. tipped her head back and yawned. "Hey, meant to tell you earlier, you did good out there tonight."

"Thanks. So did you."

On the rest of the way back to B.J.'s they talked swimming, and B.J. invited her to the pool the next day to work out.

"I'll think about that. Can I bring Nick and Carlos? Carlos loves swimming, and he's starting to open up. Maybe more time in the pool will help."

"Sounds good to me."

After dropping B.J. off, Jennie drove to the hospital. It was getting late, but she needed to see Michael. The chances of him being able to talk to her were practically zero percent, but she was in her mystery-solving mode again and had to at least try. Michael was probably the only one who could help her track down Jared. She especially wanted to find him. Even if Dad had the real arsonist, there was still the matter of the threat on her life.

Glancing in the rearview mirror, Jennie frowned at the headlights of the car behind her. She had the notion it had been there for a while—maybe since she and B.J. had left the school. When she turned in at the hospital parking lot, the vehicle, an off-white van, kept going. Jennie let out a swoosh of air. "You're way too jumpy, McGrady. Way too jumpy." She shook off the last vestiges of fear and made her way through the lighted parking garage and into the hospital.

"Hi," Jennie greeted the nurse on duty. "How's he doing?"

"No change, I'm afraid." She peered at Jennie over the rims of her glasses.

Jennie wasn't surprised but still felt a surge of disappointment. "Can I go in?"

"Have you been in to see him before?" The streaks of silver in the nurse's hair gathered light and made it look like she was wearing a halo.

"Yeah. I'm Jennie McGrady. My mom's usually—"

"Say no more." She bestowed a warm smile on Jennie. "You know the procedure." While Jennie got into the clean gown and accessories, the nurse went on and on about how dedicated a woman Susan McGrady was.

"Where's Mrs. Winslow?" Jennie asked. "Mom said she would be staying here tonight."

"Oh, she is. I sent her down to take a break while we changed his dressings. She should be back soon."

Suited up and feeling like an alien in all that mint green, Jennie quietly slipped into Michael's room.

"Hi." She sat in the chair. His eyes were closed, his body still. He reminded her of a dead person she'd seen at an open-coffin funeral once. Only the corpse had looked better. Jennie tried not to think about that. Instead she focused on a clear drop of IV solution as it escaped the bottle and dripped into the IV tube. *Drip. Drip. Drip.*

"The police arrested Marissa Cole today," she said. "Thought you might like to know."

If she'd expected some kind of reaction to her news, she didn't get it. Jennie thought again about the vision and wondered about the strangeness of it all. Had Michael really died that day? Was his body just an empty shell and had his soul already winged its way to heaven? She'd heard that in a song once. Was he already up in heaven having a great time with God? Or was he trapped in his body? She didn't know much about such things. Wasn't sure she wanted to know. Maybe no one knew for sure. How could they? You'd have to die to find out, and then you couldn't tell anybody.

"Where are you, Michael?" Jennie sighed. "I wish I knew if you could hear me. I need to know where I can find Jared. I need to know why his brother thinks the police are still holding him and why they want to kill me."

Drip. Drip. Drip. The solution fell like tears.

Jennie swallowed hard, pushed back the chair, and paced across the floor. "None of this is making any sense. Someone is setting up Marissa. They must be. Is it Jared's brother? Rich Rienhardt. Do you know about him?" She stopped and came back over beside the bed and gripped the rail. "How can I help Jared if I can't find him?"

Jennie closed her eyes and tried to pray. No words would come. Her thoughts wouldn't settle down enough to be spoken.

The door opened and another green alien walked in. "Hi, Jennie." Maddie Winslow slipped an arm around Jennie's shoulder. "What are you doing out so late?"

"What time is it?"

"Quarter after ten."

"Ouch. Guess I'd better go." Jennie reached the door and turned around. "Thanks for taking over for my mom tonight."

Maddie nodded. "It's the least I can do, Jennie. You be careful driving home, okay?"

"I will."

Jennie dragged off her greens and practically ran out of the hospital. She hated the helpless feeling she got being around Michael. There didn't seem to be anything she or anyone could do to help him.

Stuffing her hands deep in her pockets, Jennie shivered. It had cooled off again—definitely felt like fall. And here she was without a jacket again. She crossed the street and headed into the lighted parking garage.

Tires screeched and squealed on the pavement. A van ground to a stop in front of her. A truck stopped behind her. Flashes of white from two sets of high-beam headlights surrounded her. Scuffling footsteps. Car doors slammed—two, maybe three.

"Get her!" a deep voice shouted.

Something struck her head from behind. Sudden darkness.

It happened too quickly for Jennie to be frightened. Fear didn't enter the picture until much later when she woke up in a strange bed in a strange house. And even then she was more curious than afraid. The thing that brought on the raging torrents of fear and the feeling of doom was the nylon rope that bound her hands and feet together. And seeing Rich Reinhardt's shaved head and pebble-hard eyes not more than a foot from her face.

17

Jennie jerked back and tried to sit up. Her head felt like it had been used as a soccer ball.

"Hey." Rich smiled. His smooth voice was the kind of tone a guy might use with his date. As near as Jennie could remember, he hadn't asked—and she definitely hadn't accepted. "I'm sorry about the bump on the head. Told the guys not to rough you up too much."

"Where am I?" Jennie's throat felt tight and dry. She pushed herself to a sitting position.

He chuckled and pulled a chair around, straddling it, his arms draped across the back. "Now, you don't expect me to tell you that, do you?"

"Why—?"

"Didn't you get my note?" He rested his chin on his arms. He might have been handsome if not for the aura of evil that surrounded him.

"Jared . . ." Jennie swallowed back a rising panic.

"Right. I want my brother back. No more games." His tone was clipped now, edges hard and sharp as razor blades.

They don't have him, she started to say, then stopped herself, again feeling the need to protect Jared. "You won't get away with this."

He laughed again. "You're funny, Jennie girl." His eyes were the color of blue ice. His features sharp and chiseled.

Up close he didn't resemble Jared much at all. Rich was older—by about ten years. Jared had a warmth and sincerity that Rich only pretended to have. "I'm sure Lieutenant McGrady will see the light."

Jennie swallowed hard, forcing back the bile that rose to her throat. "What makes you think the police have him?"

"I have my sources."

Your sources aren't too reliable. "Are you . . . planning to kill me?"

"Maybe." He grinned. "Maybe not. Depends on whether or not your dad comes through for me."

Jennie closed her eyes, debating whether or not to tell Rich that his little brother no longer wanted to be a part of his disgusting organization. She doubted he'd believe her. Part of her wanted to taunt him, to tell him his brother had chosen the higher path. But Jennie sensed he'd kill her on the spot. Her best chance of survival, she decided, was silence and to hope that Dad would find Jared.

In the meantime she'd have to stay calm and alert to any opportunity to escape. Opening her eyes again, Jennie's gaze slid back to her captor. He was still studying her as though some secret code were etched across her forehead. A cold chill passed through her.

He stood and pushed the chair aside. Snatching a knife from a leather holster on his belt, he pressed a knee on the bed and reached for her.

Jennie flinched when he brought the knife down. She bit her lip to keep from screaming. "No need for these." Rich slid the knife between her hands and sliced through the ropes and slipped the knife back in its sheath.

Not daring to speak, Jennie released the breath she'd been holding and rubbed the sore, reddened skin on her wrists.

"Thought you might like something to eat." Rich grabbed her arm and hauled her off the bed. "Don't get any ideas about escaping. You won't. This place is as tight as an army compound."

After feeding her a breakfast of eggs, ham, and toast, Rich gave her a tour. The house was an older two-bedroom log cabin with a loft. The kitchen, living, and dining areas were all part of a great room with high windows that offered a view of fir trees and, in the distance, a mountain—Jennie wasn't certain which one. It wasn't pointy enough for Mount Hood and too tall to be Mount St. Helens. Maybe Mount Adams in Washington State. Outside, half a dozen men in camouflage fatigues milled around—some carried weapons, some seemed occupied with various chores.

"I expect you to earn your keep while you're staying with us," Rich said. "Keep the house clean, do the dishes, and cook meals—you can cook, can't you?"

Jennie stared at him without answering. He wasn't a big man—maybe only a couple inches taller than she. She straightened, teeth clenched. He may have captured her, but she did not plan on helping him or his men.

He laughed again. "Oh, Jennie girl. I can see we're going to have to have a little talk." Picking up a rifle, he grabbed her arm and pulled her across the wood floor and out onto the porch. "Kids are supposed to obey their elders."

Panic spread through her again like a forest fire. Terrified, she hooked her arm around the support beam, jerking them both to a stop. "Where are you taking me?"

"You obviously don't like my first plan, so I'm showing you the alternative." He yanked her to him, nearly pulling her arm out of its socket. "We've got a little prison of sorts—nothing fancy. Maybe a few hours in there will take some of that stubbornness out of you." He snorted. "Sure worked for Jared."

When Jennie dug in her heels and pulled her arm out of

his grasp, Rich yelled for one of the men working on a truck to help him. The ruckus set off a chain of barks and growls from the pen that held four big Rotweilers. One man at each side, they dragged her across the yard. When they reached a small shed, Rich handed his rifle to his buddy and slammed Jennie up against the wall. His face not more than an inch away, he used his entire body to pin her to the wood. "You won't do that again, Jennie girl," he growled. "Not if you want to get out of this alive." He pressed his arm against her throat. "Do I make myself clear?"

Jennie swallowed hard, determined not to cry. Rich took her silence for a yes, released her, and shoved her inside. The force propelled her across the dirt floor. She struck her shoulder and head against the wall on the opposite side of the small room. The heavy door closed and a lock clicked into place.

"Let me out of here!" Jennie tore back across the room and banged her fists against the door.

"When you're ready to cooperate." Rich laughed. Through a pencil-thin opening between the boards, Jennie watched them walk away.

"When do you want us to let her out?" the man who'd helped him asked.

"*I'll* let her out when I'm good and ready. The girl needs to know her place."

"That'll do it. You think the cops will turn Jared loose?"

"Let's hope so. Don't much like the thought of killing a white girl."

"Aarrgh!" Jennie beat on the door again. "You racist pigs."

Settle down, McGrady, she told herself. *Getting mad isn't going to help*. Jennie grabbed the door handle. It slid down but the door didn't budge. They'd used a padlock. She leaned back against it, taking several long, deep breaths. *Defying Rich was a stupid thing to do. You should have gone along with him. At least then you could have scoped the place out. It may be heavily guarded, but you might have been able to find a way out. Now you're stuck.*

As rage melted and terror subsided, a sense of hopelessness washed over her and with that came tears. "What am I going to do now, God?" Jennie whispered. She sank to her knees in the damp black earth, grabbed a handful, squeezed it into a clump, and threw it against the far wall. It smelled musty and old. The wetness seeped into her jeans. "How can you let those creeps get away with this?"

Jennie had asked that question more often than she cared to remember. She'd heard the answer often enough. Everyone would stand before God one day and would have to answer to Him for all the wrong they've done. "Maybe knowing that should be enough, God, but it isn't." Jennie wanted justice now. That's part of why she wanted to be in law enforcement like her dad and Gram. Not that God needed help in rounding up criminals. Jennie believed He used police officers and agents to bring about justice.

She sighed. Sitting there philosophizing about the judgment of evil people wasn't going to get her out of there. Okay, so she was stuck in a decaying old shed. That didn't mean she shouldn't try to escape. Maybe she could pry loose some boards.

She tried them all, but the only things she managed to move were the thick, sticky spider webs that draped the walls and filled the corners. The unpainted building had weathered and every board was hard as stone. Light squeezed in through the thin openings between some of the boards. There were holes in the roof, but no way of reaching them. Except for her and a piece of plywood in the center of the room, the square little building was empty. Jennie suspected it had once been a pump house and that the board covered a well. Her curiosity being what it was, Jennie lifted a corner of the wood. A black hole some two feet across confirmed her suspicions. Grabbing another handful of dirt and pressing it into a clod, she tossed it into the yawning hole and waited. She heard a faint splash a few seconds later as the dirt hit water.

Something tore out of the hole and scurried across the floor. Jennie stifled a scream and dropped the board. *It's a mouse, McGrady.* Jennie backed up to the wall. *Just a little mouse. You are not afraid of mice.*

Oh, great. Now she was hyperventilating. Jennie pulled the bottom of her T-shirt loose and held it against her nose and mouth, then concentrated on taking slow, deep breaths. She closed her eyes, trying to imagine the cute little mouse in the Tom and Jerry cartoons rather than the giant sewer rat her brain had brought to mind. She watched the mouse run around the room, probably more terrified than she.

Jennie lowed her T-shirt, then took pity on the little guy and lifted up the board, just enough for him to run back in. She adjusted the board, making certain every inch of the well was covered. She just hoped the ground around her remained solid and that the mouse and his friends and family hadn't created too many tunnels.

"You gotta get out of here," she murmured.

Grabbing another handful of dirt, Jennie hit on an idea. Maybe she could dig her way out. There was a cement foundation, but with any luck at all she could burrow her way under it. After scoping out the area as best she could, Jennie went to the back wall and began digging. The shed stood only a few feet from a barn. Every once in a while she could hear the snorts and soft whinnies of the horses. She didn't see that many men around. Maybe five or six besides Rich. They all wore camouflage uniforms and carried weapons. None of them had gone into the barn so far. She'd burrow out, then wait until dark to escape. She'd easily be able to sneak into the barn, take one of the horses, and ride away.

Jennie's empathy for Jared doubled over the next six hours as she worked. She wondered how often he'd been stuck in there as punishment and for how long. Unfortunately, the dirt had only been soft for about six inches. Now she was into rocks and soil nearly as hard as the concrete itself.

The hole she'd dug was about a foot across and at least that deep, but she still hadn't cleared the foundation. She leaned back on her heels and wiped her sweaty brow with her forearm. The sound of approaching footsteps sent her heart skittering. Jennie wished God would magically open a door for her to run into like she'd done for the mouse. She glanced at the door, then back at the hole she'd dug. She didn't want to think about what Rich would do if he discovered it.

Click. Rich put the key in the lock. "You ready to try this again, Jennie girl?"

Jennie shoved the loose dirt back into the hole.

Click. Scrape. He pulled the lock out of the metal clasp.

Jennie stepped on the dirt, packing down the mound.

Wood scraped against wood as Rich pulled at the door.

Jennie moved to the side wall and sat cross-legged on the floor.

"What's the matter, Jennie girl? Cat got your tongue? I asked you a question." He struck the rifle against her foot.

Jennie debated answering him. If she didn't, maybe he'd leave her in the shed and she could keep working on the hole. With as little progress as she'd made thus far, she might not get a hole dug for days. If she went along with him, she might have a better chance.

"I . . ."

"I can't hear you." He grabbed a handful of her hair and yanked her head back.

"Don't, please . . ." The pain brought tears to her eyes. "I'll do what you want."

"That's better." He let go of her and, grabbing her arm, yanked her up.

He prodded her with the business end of the rifle as he

herded her into the house. When they got to the porch, he shoved her inside. "Go get yourself cleaned up. You look like you've been sleeping in a pig sty."

I'm not nearly as dirty as you are, Jennie felt like saying. *At least my dirt will wash off*. Instead she said, "I don't have anything else to wear."

"Stupid broad." He leaned his rifle against the door frame, grabbed her wrist, and pulled her across the living room and up the stairs to the loft. "This is Jared's room. He's not much bigger than you. You should be able to find something in here. There's a washer and dryer downstairs next to the bathroom. Figure it out. Then I want you down in the kitchen. There's food in the fridge and instructions on the counter. Screw up and you're back in the pump house."

He dropped her wrist as if she had some kind of skin disease and stomped off. Jennie watched him from the loft until he'd taken his rifle and gone outside.

When she could no longer see him, Jennie dug through Jared's closet. There wasn't much to choose from. Two sets of fatigues, a pair of jeans, and a camouflage T-shirt. She picked the jeans and T-shirt and took them into the bathroom. Locking the door, Jennie took a long, hot shower, washing away the dirt and the crawling places on her skin where Rich had touched her. The dirt came off, the crawling sensation on her skin and the disgust in her heart didn't.

For the next two days, Jennie cooked and cleaned, did laundry for Rich and his small army, and fed the horses and dogs. The men didn't socialize much—at least not with her, but she was gleaning some information. Enough, she thought, to testify against them if—no, *when* she could escape. Believing themselves to be the pure race, they sought to eliminate the enemy and actually used the Bible to back up their views. She had learned one thing that could possibly help her escape. Rich actually believed that if she hung around long enough, she'd come around to his way of thinking. Jennie decided to put that misconception to good use.

Jennie set a large platter of roast beef on the table, along with mashed potatoes, gravy, and green beans in an onion bacon sauce. The men made their usual noises about how good the food was, and after Rich asked a blessing, they dug in.

The table prayers had surprised her at first. When she'd asked Rich about it afterward he'd acted like she was some kind of heathen. "We believe in the Good Book and all its teachings. We also believe the government has gone too far in taking away our rights. We believe in the right to bear arms and to own land without all these restrictions. And we think we ought to be able to get jobs based on our qualifications instead of our sex or the color of our skin. We don't think Blacks and Hispanics, or Asians, Indians, and gays should be getting special privileges. It's getting so a white guy can't get a job anymore 'cause the government says you gotta meet a quota. Don't matter if you're qualified—what counts is if you're a minority."

"Maybe some of that is unfair, but—"

"I know what you're going to say. We should take our concerns to Washington." He sneered. "Fat lot of good that does. They don't understand our mission." He'd walked away then, as if he'd answered her question. He hadn't, of course; he'd only left her with more.

Jennie sat at the end of the table opposite Rich, nearest the kitchen. She looked around at the men, each of whom she now knew by name. Rather, by nickname. Bones sat to her right. The tall, skinny man from the Midwest had been a farmer forced off his farm when the government refused him disaster relief after a flood in which his wife and most of his livestock had died. Jennie felt sorry for Bones—for all of the men, actually. She just couldn't understand why they would join an Aryan group like Rich's.

Silver, whose hair would have been that if it hadn't been shaved off, was a member of the NRA. He vowed never to give up his right to bear arms and would go to his grave defending that right. Jennie believed as her parents did in some form of gun control but didn't dare say so.

Next was Jesse, then Rich and Billy. Jesse and Billy were brothers who'd done time for robbing a bank. They hadn't told Jennie why they'd joined, only that they were angry with the system.

Thoreau—so named because of his love for poetry—sat next to Billy. On the first night she'd cooked for them, Thoreau had shared from his journal of poems. He'd been a political-science professor at some big university—she didn't know which and he hadn't said. Nor had he told her what had gone wrong, only that he had been accused of something and arrested. He'd been innocent, he said, but the FBI had released word of his arrest to the press. "My reputation was ruined, Jennie. I was tried and convicted long before the trial. I blame the FBI for that."

"Hey, Rich," Texas, a big man from the same state, drawled. "I'm startin' to think maybe we should forget Jared and move on to Idaho. Take Jennie here with us. She's much better lookin' and—ooowie—can that girl cook!"

Fear lodged like a bone in the back of her throat. She pretended not to notice the way Rich looked at her or the way he seemed to be mulling it over, chewing on his steak like a cow with his cud.

"We'll wait for Jared and take Jennie too," he finally said. "How about it, Jennie girl? Now that you know what we're all about?"

It took every ounce of courage Jennie had not to bolt from the table. It took even more to look Rich in the eye. "I might be interested. But only if you let me carry a weapon."

Texas guffawed and slapped her on the back. "Kid's

tough as nails, Reinhardt. Maybe you ought to take her up on it."

"What are you guys, crazy?" Jesse speared his bloody steak. "She's a cop's kid, for cripes sake. We shouldn't have taken her in the first place."

Jennie went on cutting her meat as though she hadn't heard him.

"Which is why we can't let her go." Rich scowled at Jesse. "Don't matter whether the cops release Jared or not. Bottom line is, Jennie stays with us—or she dies."

18

"Oh, Dad, I'm so scared." She breathed the words, too frightened to whisper lest someone hear. "Where are you? Why haven't you found me?"

Jennie stared at the stars that hung in the inky black sky outside the now dark cabin. She must have dreamed up a hundred escape plans and discarded every one of them. Rich stayed in the downstairs bedroom beneath the loft, his rifle always within reach. Jesse guarded the front of the house—Billy the back. Though Jennie hadn't responded to Rich's ultimatum at the dinner table, he must have known what she was thinking because he had added a third guard, Texas, to stand watch out by the vehicles and patrol the periphery. The other men were in the bunkhouse.

Jennie had hoped that her compliance would make the men more lax. It hadn't. She couldn't make a move outside of the house without being watched. Still, Jennie refused to give up. Nighttime offered the best chance of escape. In fact, she'd worn her shirt and jeans to bed every night, in the off chance an opportunity should arise. There had been none.

The other thing she'd hoped to do was to find out if Rich and his men had burned down Trinity. She'd brought up the subject half a dozen times, and all the response she'd gotten was that they thought Reverend Cole's arrest was hilarious. "Serves her right," Rich had said. The fact that they hadn't bragged about their conquest made Jennie seriously doubt their involvement. On the other hand, they hadn't denied it either.

As she closed her eyes, another plan began to unfold. Tomorrow night she'd stay awake. Then pretending she couldn't sleep, she'd bring a plate of brownies and milk to the night guards. On her way from one to another, she'd slip away. She'd made friends with several of the horses the last two days. They were pastured behind the barn. She'd lure one of them, probably Missy, a beautiful Arabian mare, to the far end of the field. Then would come the tricky part of getting the horse to jump the fence. She imagined herself mounting Missy. She'd grab hold of the mane, lean forward, get her going at a full run, then sail over the barbed-wire fence to freedom.

With that thought, Jennie fell asleep.

Sometime later, Jennie awoke with a start. It was still dark, but something was definitely wrong. She'd heard something. There it was again, a faint creaking sound. The kind the stairs made when she climbed them. A dark figure approached her bed. She started to scream. His hand shot out and covered her mouth.

"Don't make a sound," he hissed, then leaned closer. "I'm not going to hurt you."

Jennie squinted, trying to make out his features. Moonlight glinted off his shaved blond head. Rich? No, *Jared.*

He drew back his hand and Jennie scooted up in bed. "What are you doing here?"

"Get dressed," he whispered, "we're getting—"

The living room lights came on. "Get your hands up." Rich cocked the rifle and trained it on Jared. "Turn around so I can see you."

Jared slowly raised his hands and turned to face his

brother. "Hey, bro—what kind of greeting is that?"

"Jared?" Rich lowered his gun. "What are you doing up there?"

"Me? What's she doing up here? This is my bedroom, remember?" Jared glanced back at Jennie, then down at Rich. "The cops finally decided to let me go. I would have been here sooner but it took me a while to lose them."

"You sure you lost 'em?"

"I'm sure. Pretty stupid, if you ask me." Jared started for the stairs. Jennie shrank back into the bed. She felt certain Jared had come to get her. Was he lying about losing the police? Was Dad here somewhere? Her hopes soared.

The front door opened and Jesse came in. "Everything okay in here?"

"Yeah," Rich said. "No thanks to you. Why weren't you at your post?"

"Something spooked the horses. Went out with Texas to check. Didn't see nothin'. Came back and saw the lights was on." His gaze drifted to Jared. "How'd you get in here?"

Jared shrugged and descended the stairs. "Just walked in. Must have been me that set the horses off. I came in on the south road. Sorry about that. Guess I should have let you all know I was back. Didn't want to wake anyone. Figured I'd just hit the sack and talk to you in the morning."

"Good to see you, kid." Rich slung an arm around Jared's neck. "You guys better get back out there. Knowing cops, they may have had more than one tail." He released Jared and walked Jesse to the door. "Get the others up. I want the grounds searched. Use the dogs."

"I told you I lost them," Jared said. "Don't you believe me?"

Rich lifted the curtain and peered outside. "Yeah, I believe you, I just don't trust McGrady. He's going to want his daughter back."

Jared whistled, his gaze moving to the loft. "That's Jennie?"

"Who'd you think it was?"

Jared shrugged. "A new recruit—I don't know. Why is she here?"

"Told McGrady we'd make an exchange. Jennie for you. Didn't the cops tell you?"

"Are you kidding? They just handed me my stuff and told me to get out." Jared rubbed a hand across his newly shaved hair. "I was really careful, Rich. Took the old road and cut off into the woods for a couple miles."

Jennie's heart constricted. What was going on? Had Jared really come to get her out? Or had he just come back? What kind of game was Jared playing? And where was Dad?

"Don't worry about it," Rich said. "If anybody followed you in here, they won't live to see the sunrise."

Jared nodded and looked up into the loft, sending her a warning to play along. Or was it just a look of contempt? Jennie couldn't be sure.

"You want your bed back?" Rich offered. "We can kick Jennie out and give her the sofa."

Jared shook his head. "Naw, leave her there for tonight. Sofa's too close to the door. And to tell you the truth, after tonight I don't much trust the guys to make sure she doesn't get loose."

"You're right about that. I need to get a few more men up here."

"Ah . . . Rich," Jared said as he dropped onto the couch, "now that I'm back, what are you planning to do with Jennie?"

Rich explained the options. "Kill her or take her along to Idaho."

"I vote for killing her." Jared scowled as he glanced up at the loft.

The words ripped into Jennie's heart like a hunting knife. What was he doing?

Rich came back and stood over his brother, arms folded. "Do I detect a little resentment here?"

"It's Jennie's fault I landed in jail. She turned me in for setting that fire."

Another lie. She'd only reported him being on the scene after the fire.

"So you did set it. I wondered." Rich seemed pleased. Jennie felt sick.

"Yeah, I set it. And I planted evidence so that black pastor would take the fall. Went back the next day to finish it up and Jennie saw me. I want her to die, Rich, and I want to be the one to do it."

"Hoowie! You are growing up, boy. I was beginning to think you didn't have it in you." Rich punched his brother in the shoulder. "Okay, I'll miss her cooking, but you're right. She's trouble. Best to get her out of the way."

"Good. I'll take her out in the morning. Maybe one of the guys can ride along to help me dig the grave."

Rich laughed, sending cold chills up Jennie's spine. "You hear that, Jennie girl? Better say your prayers. Looks like tonight was your last supper."

Long after the lights were out, Jennie lay staring into the night sky, trying to make sense of what she'd heard. Was Jared really going to kill her? She shuddered again at their cold, calculating discussion, as if killing her were no more a moral issue than hunting down and killing a deer. She desperately wanted to believe that Jared had come to sneak her out of the compound. Now she was thoroughly confused. If he meant to help her, why had he suggested to Rich that she be killed and why had he wanted one of the other men to come along—unless he really did want someone to help dig her grave?

The sun rose despite Jennie's prayers that it wouldn't. Jared had come in around two in the morning. Jennie slept in snatches after that, awakening again and again to dogs barking in the distance. And once, the sound of gunfire. She practically flew out of bed. Who had they killed? Though the thought it might be Dad waited on the periphery of her consciousness, she refused to entertain it.

She wavered between being terrified and being angry. By morning she felt numb. All through breakfast, Jennie listened and watched and hoped and prayed for the cavalry to ride in and take the camp by storm. Every law-enforcement agency in the state had to know she was in danger. So why didn't they come?

She peered out the window again. Texas and Bones were standing by the victim of the gunshot she'd heard early that morning. Though the sight of the deer hanging in the yard, gutted and cooling, made her want to puke, she was thankful it wasn't a human. Jennie piled the last of the pancakes onto a platter in the oven. She marveled at her acting abilities as she went out to the porch and rang the bell. One by one the guys straggled in. Jennie set platters of pancakes, eggs, and ham on the table, then sat down next to Jared, who'd squeezed in an extra chair.

They all bowed their heads while Rich said grace. Jennie's anger came back full force. "You hypocrites," she said aloud. She hadn't meant to, but now it was too late. She pushed herself away from the table.

"Did you say something?" Rich fixed his icy glare on her, daring her to continue.

Jennie looked around at the men. Texas shot her a warning glance. She'd be nailing holes in her coffin, but what did it matter? One way or another she was going to die. She might as well have her say. "How can you call yourselves Christians? You're nothing but cold-blooded killers. You think God would condone what you're doing? You're crazy." Jennie stepped back. She could almost feel the heat of Rich's fury as he watched her. He said nothing as she continued.

"The Gospel teaches that we are to love one another. You people don't know what love is. And I don't want to spend another second looking at you." Jennie took another step back, then straightened and turned, marched through the living room, and ascended the stairs.

The silence stretched on until Jennie thought she'd explode. Would Rich come after her and beat her senseless? She dropped onto the unmade bed.

"You gonna let her get away with that?" Jesse asked.

Rich laughed. "Don't worry about it. Jared and I are taking her out and burying her this morning."

Less than an hour later, Jennie stood next to the Arabian with Jared on one side, Rich on the other. They mounted their horses and grabbed for Jennie's reins at the same time.

"Great minds . . ." Jared flashed his brother a grin.

Rich chuckled and withdrew his hand. "You two go ahead. I'll bring up the rear."

Jared moved his gelding out, pulling Missy alongside. Rich didn't trust him, Jennie could tell. That should have made her feel better, but it didn't. She didn't trust Jared either.

All during the hour-long ride, Jennie imagined herself taking back the reins and spurring Missy on, dodging trees, outrunning her captors. She visualized Jared getting the drop on Rich and giving her a chance to run. She even imagined herself using karate to punch and kick her abductors like she'd seen Gram do once. Only problem was, Jennie didn't know karate.

"Stop here." Rich pulled up his horse.

"You sure this is far enough from the house?" Jared turned his and Jennie's horses around.

"Don't matter. We'll be gone by morning." Rich drew his rifle out of his saddle holster, then unhooked two shovels from his pack. "We'll bury her here."

"Whatever." Jared dismounted and came around to help Jennie down. She was on the ground when he whispered in her ear, "I'm sorry. It wasn't supposed to be like this."

Jennie turned around, looking into his sad blue eyes. He *had* come back to rescue her. Now they were both trapped.

"Start digging, kids." Rich cocked the rifle. "Only, make the hole big enough for two."

19

"W-what are you talking about?" Jared stammered. "I'm not—"

"Save it. Don't you think I know a traitor when I see one? You lied about setting that fire. I thought all along you might have. Figured all those visits there were so you could scope the place out. That's why I made sure the black broad would take the rap for it. I'm the one who planted the evidence." He shook his head. "You disappoint me, boy." He jammed the barrel into Jared's ribs. "Dig."

The grave would be a shallow one. Jennie and Jared had only gotten about a foot down with all the roots to dig around. Her fury had dissipated with each shovelful. Now, except for the raw blisters on her hand, she felt numb again and too tired to care. Jared kept tossing angry looks at her as though his brother's decision to kill them both was her fault.

Jennie leaned against the shovel, tired of the work and the silence and asked, "How could you kill your own brother?"

"I hope you're not going to start preaching at me again, Jennie girl. I know the Bible. In the first book, Cain kills Abel. There's lots of killin' in the Bible, for your information. God did a good portion of it himself trying to purify the earth. That's what we're all about, Jennie. Helping God purify the world by getting rid of the garbage."

"Garbage. Meaning people who don't think like you or

have the same color skin?" Jennie closed her eyes. The man was insane.

"There's no use arguing with him." Jared shoved his blade deep into the ground.

"He's right there, Jennie girl." Rich stood and stretched. "You two keep digging. I got to take me a little walk into the bushes. Don't get any ideas about running. I'll have you in my sights the whole time."

Jared watched him until he was out of earshot, then turned back to Jennie. "You need to get out of here. Go as soon as Rich gets behind the bushes. If you run due east of here you'll get to Wind River campground. I was supposed to meet your dad and some FBI agents there."

"You were working with my dad?"

"Yeah. It's a long story." He glanced over his shoulder. "Go—now!"

Ripples of sunlight danced through the trees, making the clearing seem peaceful and serene. Yet none of that peace reached Jennie. "What about you? Rich will kill you. . . ."

"Don't worry about me. Just get out of here. Go!"

Jennie hesitated for a moment, then dropped her shovel and ran. She'd gotten only a short distance when she turned around. *You can't leave Jared.* She debated going for help and directing the FBI agents back here, but it would be too late by then. Rich would be furious. Jared might stand a chance if she could outwit Rich.

A gunshot echoed through the dense forest. Jennie ducked, covering her mouth to silence her screams. Rich had killed him. Shots erupted again. *No, it can't be Rich,* she reasoned. The shots were too far away. "The compound." Maybe the cavalry had come. Maybe Dad and the others had rushed them when Jared hadn't come back. Maybe . . . Another possibility came to mind—that the heavily armed men with the shaved heads might win.

Jennie shook off the thought. She needed to get back to

Jared. As she circled back to the would-be grave site, Jennie picked up and discarded several sticks she planned to use against Rich. She envisioned Jared keeping him occupied while she snuck up behind Rich, using the horses as cover. She'd whack him on the head and they'd both get away.

The horses did provide cover, but as she came closer, they grew skittish and whinnied. Rich whirled around. "Hold it right there, Jennie girl. Drop the stick." He laughed. "And here I thought you were a smart kid. Shoulda run while you had the chance. Not that you'd have gotten very far. Terrain can get pretty rugged around these parts."

Jennie fought to keep her gaze on Rich and not on Jared, who moved toward his brother, shovel raised. "What can I say?" Jennie's voice dripped with sarcasm. "I missed your company." She gripped the two-inch branch even tighter.

"I said, drop—"

Jennie winced as Jared's shovel landed with a crack on the side of Rich's head. Mouth still open, a surprised look in his eyes, Rich dropped to the ground.

"Come on." Jared grabbed her hand and pulled her away. "Let's get out of here."

"No." She pulled her hand out of his grasp and knelt beside Rich, examining the bloody wound on Rich's skull. "We can't leave him like that. He needs medical attention. Help me tie him up. We'll stop the bleeding and put him on his horse."

"He deserves to die. He's—"

"That may be, Jared, but it's not our call. I wouldn't be able to live with myself if I just left him here. Could you?"

Jared sighed. "You're right. I . . . I wasn't thinking."

"Good. Now, give me your T-shirt and see if you can find some rope."

Jennie applied pressure to stop the bleeding while Jared dug a rope out of the saddlebags on Rich's horse to tie him up. Within a few minutes they had him draped over the saddle and were on their way.

"Thanks for coming back for me, Jennie," Jared said.

Jennie shrugged. "No problem. I should be the one thanking you. If you hadn't come, I'd be dead by now—or on my way to Idaho. Either way . . ." Her voice trailed away. "I have to admit, though, you had me going for a while. When you told Rich you started the fire and wanted to kill me."

Jared's lips parted in a wry smile. "I had to convince him. Unfortunately, I never was much of a liar."

Jennie frowned. "You didn't start the fire, did you?"

"No, of course not."

"Then, what were you doing snooping around the ashes the day after?"

"Trying to find the journal I'd given to Michael." He glanced back at Rich who was still out cold.

"The box?"

"Right. My journal was in it. I'd written down the names of all the members of Rich's contingent, along with crimes I knew they'd committed. They burned down those other two churches and were responsible for the cross burnings."

He looked away. "I never wanted to be part of the gang, Jennie. Never. But with Rich, you didn't say no."

"The pump house? Did he put you in it a lot?"

"That was the easiest part. At least in there I felt safe. Rich didn't believe in sparing the rod." His blue gaze met hers again. "He wasn't always like that. After Mom and Dad died, he kinda went off. It's hard to explain. They were in an accident when I was seven. Rich was fifteen. The guy driving the truck that hit them fell asleep at the wheel. He was black. Then this social worker tried to split us up. Rich went crazy. He and I ran away from a foster home one night and came to live with this great-uncle of ours. He was a member of an Aryan group."

"Where's your uncle?"

"Died a few years back. Rich buried him in the woods and kept collecting his pension check. The ranch was Uncle Bill's."

"So you told Michael all this?"

Jared nodded. "Some of it. The rest was in the journals. He seemed so easy to talk to, you know?"

"Michael's like that. Do you think your brother found out that you were talking to Michael about turning him in?"

"There's no way he could have known."

"Don't be too sure. He might have followed you," Jennie mused. "I heard Rich say he was proud of you for starting the fire, but he could have been leading you on. I mean, if he set Reverend Cole up to take the blame, doesn't it make sense that he caused the fire too?"

"At first I thought he might have, but now I don't think so. Rich looked at everything from a military standpoint. He and his men planned their hits down to the last detail. To them, the church burnings and other hits were like war maneuvers. They had maps and everything. I'd have known."

"Maybe. But if Rich thought you were leaking information, he might have kept it secret from you. He may be crazy, but he's not stupid. What if he found out about the journal and knew you were about to turn him in? He and his men could have set the fire, taken the journal, and—"

Jared shook his head. "Doesn't wash. As far as the journal goes—I'm sure Rich didn't know about that. I kept it buried in the pump house in a metal box. Other than me, Michael's the only one who ever saw it. After the fire I thought I'd better try to find it. I wasn't ready to turn it over to the police. I thought the metal would survive the fire . . . maybe it did. I don't know. You caught me before I had a chance to look."

Jennie sighed. She wanted the arsonist to be Rich. She wanted it to be over. "Why did you go to Michael in the first place?"

"Sometimes some of the guys and I would come into Portland and hang out around Pioneer Square and Old Town to recruit men for the cause. I met Michael down there. He was talking to the kids, inviting them to church and telling them God loved them—stuff like that. Something just clicked with him, you know? Hard to explain, but all of a sudden I knew he was telling the truth, and everything he said made sense. Michael gave me the courage to break away from Rich. After a few meetings, I gave Michael my journals, hoping he could help me. He said he knew a police officer we could trust. I think it was your dad. Then . . ." Jared stared off into the woods in front of them.

"Have you seen him since the fire?"

"No. I was afraid to go to the hospital. After the cops let me go that day, I hid out in Old Town. I couldn't go back to the compound."

"That's where Dad found you?"

"Well, he didn't find me, exactly. I saw on the news yesterday that you were missing and that they suspected Rich of kidnapping you. I called your dad and talked him into letting me try to get you out. He didn't want to go along with it at first, but the Feds decided to let me try—they didn't want a big confrontation. We were afraid if we stormed the place with you still there, they'd kill you for sure. The plan was for me to get you away from there. Once you were safe they'd go in."

"What happens now? To you, I mean."

"I don't know. Your dad and the DA said something about protective custody. I'll be testifying against Rich and the others."

They rode along for a while in silence. Michael had been right about Jared. Jennie just wished the youth pastor could see the results of his kindness. She also wished she could figure out who was responsible for putting Michael in the hospital. If Jared was right about his brother, she now had two fewer suspects. Jared seemed certain that Rich hadn't done it, but Jennie wasn't quite ready to cross him off the list. He was cunning and resourceful and a liar.

You're weird, McGrady, Jennie told herself. *Why are you even thinking about that? Dad's probably solved the case by now.*

"Jared?" Jennie turned toward him. "Were you in the building when the fire started?"

He hesitated, a pained expression crossing his face. "I . . . yeah. I was there. I should have stayed to help, but all I could think of was getting as far away as possible. I was afraid they'd think I did it." He looked like he was about to cry. "If I'd stayed, maybe Michael wouldn't—"

"You can't blame yourself."

He didn't respond and Jennie didn't press it. "Did you see anyone when you left?"

He shook his head. "If you mean somebody who might have started the fire, I couldn't say. I saw Michael, of course, and Reverend Cole. On my way out I saw some Mexican guy and a couple men in business suits. I didn't know them. It was pretty stupid of me to run like I did. All those witnesses putting me at the scene."

"Not at the scene. If you were there in the hallway and had just left Michael's office, you couldn't have been down in the basement setting the fire."

"Guess that's why the police let me go, huh?"

They'd come to a narrow gravel road, and Jared drew back the reins. "We're almost there. This road will take us down to the ranger station at Wind River. We should run into the deputies before that, but if not, we'll call from the ranger station." He didn't seem to want to talk the rest of the way back. That was fine with Jennie. At this point she was too tired to think straight.

A couple of sheriff's deputies were waiting at the rendezvous point. The others, as Jennie suspected, had gone into the compound.

"Sure glad to see you two," one of the deputies said. "Jennie, you have one worried father."

"I've been a little worried myself. Is he okay—I heard shooting."

"No casualties," the deputy said. "Lieutenant McGrady is on his way over here now. I'll let him know you're safe." He radioed the message to her father and while they waited asked Jennie and Jared to relate their stories.

Dad drove in fifteen minutes later. He didn't say much, just wrapped Jennie in his arms and held her like he never wanted to let go. Or maybe it was Jennie who held on.

"Oh, Dad, I was so scared. If it hadn't been for Jared . . ."

Dad released her and shook hands with Jared. After questioning them, the federal agents took Jared with them while Jennie rode back to Portland with her dad.

The compound, Jennie discovered on the long trip home, was nestled in the Mount Adams wilderness area. The men had all been arrested and there'd been only two injuries. Jesse and Billy had both been wounded in their effort to escape. The others had surrendered.

Dad about had a fit when he found out she'd escaped and turned back. But even he had to admit he'd have done the same thing. Of course, he hadn't been too happy about her getting abducted in the first place. She shouldn't have stopped at the hospital on her way home from swimming that night. She shouldn't have gone to the parking garage unescorted.

To keep Dad from lecturing her again on the subject, Jennie asked, "Have you gotten any more leads on the arson investigation? I mean, now that we know Reverend Cole didn't do it . . ."

Dad glanced over at her and frowned. "We're back to square one."

"What about the body? Do you know who—?"

He cut her off. "We're still checking that out."

Jennie sighed. "Has Carlos said anything?"

"No. At least not that I know of."

Knowing she wasn't going to get any more information out of her father, Jennie put the seat back down as far as it would go and slept the rest of the way home. She didn't wake up until they pulled into the driveway.

"Jennie! Jennie!" Nick barreled into her before she had a chance to get out of the car.

She scooped him into her arms and held him tight, burying her face in his neck.

"Why're you cryin'?" He leaned back. "Are you sad?"

Jennie sniffed and laughed. "No, I'm just glad to see you. Where's Mom?"

His deep blue gaze drifted up to the second floor. "In her room. She's sick. . . ."

Jennie shot her father a worried look, but he was already moving toward the door.

20

"When can I see my mom?" Nick tugged on Jennie's hand, pulling her into the waiting room. Carlos, silent as ever, held tightly to her other hand.

"I wish I knew." Jennie had remained behind to shower and change while Dad had literally picked Mom off the floor and taken her to the hospital. Jennie was only half an hour behind him, but worry had stretched it into an eternity.

Nick ran to Aunt Kate, who was already seated near the reception desk, and asked her the same thing. "I'm sure it won't be long." Aunt Kate lowered a *Better Homes and Gardens* magazine and pulled Nick onto her lap. "They're running some tests, so we should know something soon."

Jennie gave Carlos a hug and led him to the chair beside Kate and Nick, then paced the length of the waiting room, spun around, and paced back. "This is all my fault, Aunt Kate."

"Jennie . . ."

"No, it is. If I'd gone right home after swimming and hadn't gotten myself abducted by those creeps, this wouldn't have happened."

"She was sick before all that, honey." Kate got up and wrapped a slender arm around Jennie's shoulders. "She's been trying to do too much." She sighed. "With Michael and family and—"

"Me. How is he?" Jennie asked. "Did his sister come?"

"Yes. She got here yesterday. Ashley hasn't left his side since she arrived."

Jennie glanced at her watch. "Do you think I'd have time to go see him?"

"Go ahead. I'll have you paged if we hear anything."

Jennie raced up to the burn unit, slowing when she neared Michael's room. A woman wearing a pastel blue dress was slipping her arms into the drab green gown. Her flaxen hair was pulled back in a bun, and tendrils of curls framed her tan face. She tucked it all into the green cap. Glancing up, she caught Jennie's gaze and smiled, motioning her inside.

Jennie donned the all-too-familiar green isolation garb and went into the room.

"You must be Jennie." She spoke with a slight British accent.

"How did you know?"

"Oh, your mum told me all about you. We've been praying for you. I'm glad to see our prayers have been answered. I'm Michael's sister, Ashley Montgomery."

Jennie nodded. "I'm glad you're here."

"I wish I could have come sooner. We were in the field and didn't get the message right away."

At Jennie's puzzled look, Ashley went on to explain. "My husband, Brent, and I run an orphanage and a hospital in Tanzania. We go out to the villages and care for the people who are too ill or weak to come to us."

"Sounds interesting."

"It is. You will have to come visit sometime." Ashley glanced out into the hallway. "Where is your mother? She said she'd be by today."

Jennie told her about coming home and finding Mom passed out again. "She's been sick off and on for a couple weeks."

"Oh, I didn't know. She seemed fine yesterday. Worried about you, of course, but . . ."

"How is Michael?" Jennie asked, changing the subject.

Ashley's soft blue gaze shifted to her brother's face. "No change, I'm afraid. I wish I could have come sooner . . . before . . . but then, it does no good to make wishes after the fact, does it?"

Jennie forced herself to look at his permanently scarred face. "You were right about Jared, Michael," she said. "You were right to trust him." Turning to Ashley, she added, "Do you think he can hear me?"

"I wouldn't be surprised." She smiled. "Would you like to tell me about this Jared? I'd like to hear a bit about what my brother's been up to. Your mother shared a great deal, but I'd like to hear more."

"Sure. Michael was counseling him. . . ." Jennie went on to tell her about Jared and the fire and how Michael had been a hero. She also told Ashley about the day Michael had coded. "I thought for sure he'd died. I saw this—" Jennie stopped. "I'm sorry. I shouldn't be talking about that."

Ashley placed her slender hand on Jennie's. "Please, go on. What did you see?"

"I thought I saw Michael die. It was so weird. I didn't want him to—but it was like a movie playing in my mind. He even said good-bye. It was like he wanted to go."

Tears glistened in Ashley's eyes. "Oh, Jennie, I can't tell you how relieved I am. It helps me know what I must do."

"I don't understand."

"As you probably know, the doctors don't offer much hope for Michael's recovery. They've asked me to consider taking him off life support. At first I wouldn't hear of it. Now that I've been with him . . ." She sighed. "I have prayed and struggled and this morning I agreed. Bless you, Jennie. Your story has confirmed to me that I'm doing the right thing.

We'll take him off life support and leave him completely in God's hands."

Jennie barely heard her name being paged over the turmoil of emotions tumbling around inside her. She didn't want Michael to die but knew in her heart that Ashley was right. "I . . . I'd better go," Jennie stammered. "My mom . . ."

"Oh yes, by all means. You'll let me know—about your mother, I mean?"

Jennie nodded.

"And don't worry, Jennie. God will take care of Michael—whether it's here on earth or up in heaven."

Jennie believed that, too, but it didn't make things any easier. Why did things have to be so complicated? Jennie wished more than anything she could go back to the days before the fire. Things had changed so much, she doubted they'd ever get back to the way they were.

By the time Jennie reached the emergency room, Kate, Nick, and Carlos were gone.

"We've admitted her," the receptionist said, looking over her half glasses and smiling. "Room 312. Your father said to send you up."

Jennie went back to the elevator and punched the up arrow. When the elevator doors opened, she stepped inside, immediately recognizing the only other occupant. "Mr. Beaumont. Hi."

"Jennie! What—I mean, I thought you were—I saw on television . . ."

Jennie had to smile at his obvious shock. That and his resemblance to a guppy as his mouth opened and closed. As long as she'd known him he'd never been at a loss for words.

"I'm sorry. The last I heard, you'd been abducted." He punched the button for the door to close on the elevator. It finally did and he pressed four for his floor.

Jennie pressed three and briefly filled him in on her escape.

"I see. I'm glad you're okay—the girls have been very worried. You'll have to give them a call."

"I will." She glanced down at the bouquet of pink carnations and baby's breath in his hand.

He held them up. "For Mrs. Talbot—from the board. I was coming over to see Michael, so I volunteered to bring them."

"How is she? I've been meaning to go see her."

"She's doing much better. They'll be transferring her to a convalescent home soon."

"Why?" The doors swished open and Jennie stepped out.

"With her injuries she'll need long-term care."

The doors closed before she could ask him any more questions. Jennie vowed to visit Mrs. Talbot before she left the hospital, then made her way to room 312. Worry for her mom settled in her stomach like a rock. It had to be serious if the doctor was keeping her there.

"I still can't believe I missed it," Kate was saying when Jennie walked in. "I guess it's been too long for both of us."

Mom laughed. "Less for me." Her face was flushed, her eyes bright.

Dad brushed a lock of hair from Mom's forehead, leaned over the bed rail, and kissed her. "Well, I'm just glad we found out what's been going on."

Jennie looked from one to the other. Judging from the grins on their faces, the news must be good.

"What *is* going on?" Jennie approached the bed.

"Oh, Jennie." Mom reached up for a hug. "Welcome home. I was worried sick."

Join the crowd. "I'm okay, Mom." Jennie pulled out of Mom's embrace. "I've been kind of worried about you too."

Nick bounced out of his chair. "Guess what . . . Mom's—what's that word again, Daddy?"

"Pregnant." Dad fastened his warm gaze back on Mom. She touched a finger to his cheek, then looked back at Jennie.

Tears blurred Jennie's vision.

"That means we're going to have a baby." Nick raised his arms for Dad to hold him.

"I know what it means, Nick," Jennie snapped as she tightened her grip on the bed rail.

"What's wrong, sweetheart? I thought you'd be pleased." Mom reached for her.

Jennie backed away. *What is wrong with you, McGrady? This is the part where you're supposed to jump up and down for joy and dance around in circles. Mom's okay. She's having a baby.*

But Jennie didn't feel like dancing or jumping or anything else. Except maybe getting away.

"Jennie, wait," Dad called after her.

Jennie ran from the room, nearly knocking down one of the nurses. She found the exit to the stairs, flew down them, taking them two and three at a time. Jennie didn't stop until she reached her car. Shoving the key into the ignition, Jennie started the Mustang and drove away. She didn't know what to do or where to go, but she had to get away before she exploded.

Half an hour later, Jennie pulled into the driveway of what had once housed her school and church. Driving past the charred remains, she parked near the gym and went inside. DeeDee sprang to her feet and gave Jennie a hug. "I heard on the news you'd been found!"

"Yep." She struggled to make her voice sound normal. "It's okay if I swim, isn't it?" She'd stopped at her house to pick up her swimsuit and leave her parents a note.

DeeDee gave her a look of understanding. "Sure. Take as long as you want."

Jennie hurried to the locker room, changed, and went back to the pool. The water simmered like an aquamarine gemstone as the afternoon sun streamed through the bank of windows on the west side.

She moved into the sunlight and rubbed the goose bumps on her arms. Taking a deep breath, she dove in.

As always, swimming helped to clear her head. She felt foolish now and frustrated with herself for reacting like she had to her mother's good news. And it *was* good. Jennie still couldn't understand why she'd behaved like such a jerk. She was no shrink but figured it had a lot to do with being kidnapped and with Michael dying and the fire.

While she swam she found herself wishing she could talk to Gram. Gram always helped her through the hard times. She'd suggest they sit at the table or in some quiet corner and have a cup of tea. Jennie imagined herself talking with Gram. Gram would probably say something like, "My goodness, darling, with all you've been through it's a wonder you're not a basket case."

"I am a basket case," Jennie would answer.

Then she might say, "You mustn't try to handle everything at once. Tuck all those problems away in little drawers in the closet of your mind. Then pull them out one at a time."

While she settled into a steady, unhurried stroke, Jennie slowed her mind as well. Piece by piece she picked her thoughts apart and set them in different drawers.

Four laps into her routine and they were all neatly tucked away. Jennie felt a surge of relief.

Now, cautiously, she opened the drawer containing what would probably be the easiest problem to resolve—the one involving her family and her new brother or sister. Why she'd reacted so strangely still upset her. She'd acted more like two than sixteen. Now she would need to apologize—especially to Mom.

Thinking back, Jennie envisioned the day she'd first learned that Mom was pregnant with Nick. Jennie had felt much the same way. Shock, anger. The last thing they needed to complicate their lives was a baby. Turned out Nick had been exactly what they needed. While no one could take Dad's place while he was missing, Nick had made Mom's and Jennie's lives more bearable.

She smiled thinking about Nick as a baby and wondered what this baby would be like. Would it be a girl or a boy? A girl, Jennie decided. Would she have dark hair like the McGradys or red like the Calhouns? Boy, girl, redhead, blonde, brunette—none of that mattered. A baby. Her heart swelled to twice its normal size. This time Dad would be there. *He will, won't he, God?*

Jennie turned, switching from a crawl to a back stroke. It was then she saw him. A figure emerging from the men's locker room, carrying a bucket and mop.

Jennie swam to the end of the pool and pushed herself up. "Rafael! Hi!"

"Hallo, Jennie. I did not see you there." He set the bucket down and came toward her.

"What are you doing with those?"

"Working. My uncle will lose his job if he cannot work. We—my father and I—come and clean for him until he comes home."

"That's very nice of you. Philippe is still in jail, then?"

"Sí. But not for the fire. Señorita Cole is causing that."

He was wrong about that, but Jennie didn't bother to correct him. "Then, why?"

"For killing the man in the basement."

21

"The man burned in the fire?"

Rafael nodded.

"Are you sure?"

"Sí. The polícia say José was dead before the fire started. My uncle could not do this. The man was his compadre—his friend."

Jennie shook her head. "This isn't making any sense. If Philippe knew him, why didn't he identify him right away?"

Rafael's Adam's apple shifted up and down. "That is why I know he did not kill him, Jennie. Philippe didn't know his friend die in the fire until the polícia tell him. Now it breaks his heart to know."

"That's terrible. How did he die?"

"Someone shoot him in head first, then start the fire to cover up. Lisa says you are a good detective. Maybe you can help Philippe. My uncle should not go to prison for something he did not do. Your father is too quick to judge Philippe and . . . you could talk to him, maybe?"

"I don't see how I can help, but, yeah, I'll ask Dad about it."

Rafael flashed her a wide smile as he thanked her, but his eyes remained dark and distressed. "Um . . . how is Carlos? Has he told you anything?"

"No. We keep hoping, but . . ." Jennie shrugged. "He and

Nick are getting pretty close, though, so maybe he'll feel comfortable enough to talk to us soon."

"I wish Mr. Beaumont would have let us keep him with us. It would have been better." He ambled back to his mop and bucket, then disappeared into the men's locker room.

Jennie turned, then pushed off from the side, gliding under the water, letting what Rafael had told her sink in. The murdered man now had an identity. He was Philippe's friend. And if Philippe hadn't killed him, who had? And why? Had Carlos seen the crime? Had he witnessed the murder? Were the arson and the murder done by the same person, or were they separate crimes?

"Those are excellent questions, Jennie," Dad said when she asked him later that evening after a dinner of take-out pizza. The boys were upstairs in bed, and Jennie and her dad were sitting on the porch swing, listening to crickets and frogs and the sounds of sunset. "But if it's all the same to you, I'd rather not talk shop."

"What do you want to talk about?"

Dad smiled. "The baby, what else? You must be feeling better about it."

Jennie nodded. When she'd finished swimming, Jennie had driven straight back to the hospital to see her mother. Mom would hardly let her apologize, just kept hugging her and crying and telling her how excited she was. The doctor wanted to keep her in the hospital overnight to run tests, one of which had been an ultrasound.

Jennie and her father talked for a while about how having a baby would be a big adjustment for everyone. Eventually, Jennie managed to steer the conversation back to Carlos and what would happen to him with his father still in jail.

"He has family, princess. I'm sure his uncle will take him.

Either that or he'll go back to Mexico to live with family there."

"Do you think Philippe killed that man?"

"I don't know. The fire has destroyed so much evidence. Half the time I feel like we're grasping at straws. I've been going over and over it. We're fairly certain now that the killer used arson to cover up his or her crime."

"Her? You don't think Reverend Cole . . . I mean, Rich said . . ."

He rubbed his eyes and dragged his hands down his face. "It's all very complicated. The fact that Rich admitted to framing her doesn't necessarily mean he did. In fact, now he says he didn't. We know she wrote those threatening letters to herself. She claims she was trying to show how terrible these groups were and at the same time call attention to the work she and the others were doing at Trinity. She swears she had nothing to do with setting the fire."

"Did she know the man who was killed?"

"Claims not to and so far we haven't made a connection."

"How do you know for sure he was murdered? Maybe the guy died accidentally." Jennie tucked her feet up under her and settled into the corner of the swing.

"Not hardly. The medical examiner discovered a bullet hole in the piece of skull found at the scene. The bullet apparently went into the back of the head."

"Oh." Jennie chewed on her lip, wondering how long Dad's mellow mood would last and how many questions she could get answers to before he told her to mind her own business. "Dad, does Marissa Cole have a gun?"

"No, but that doesn't mean she couldn't have gotten one and discarded it. She had a purse with her in the hospital, and to my knowledge it wasn't searched that night." He stretched out and set his stockinged feet on the wicker table. Tossing Jennie a crooked grin, he asked, "Why all the questions? I'd think after being held hostage for three days you'd be wiped out."

"I talked to Rafael today, and he told me about the man being Philippe's friend. He doesn't think his uncle did it."

"I know. He told us that, too, but we have to look at the evidence. We figure Philippe was using the church basement to operate a business on the side. He and his friend, whom we now have identified as José Chavez, were bringing illegal immigrants into the country and supplying them with falsified papers and green cards. They would get them jobs and take a percentage of their paychecks as payment. We've tracked down two families who have come in that way."

"Not Rafael's family?"

"No, they're legal. Beaumont had his lawyer check them all out."

"What about Philippe's friend?"

"The immigration office has no record of him even applying. He was working for a Mexican restaurant in Tigard. That's where we found the two illegals. I'm betting José and Philippe disagreed on something and Philippe shot him. Carlos may have witnessed it and is afraid to say anything for fear it will incriminate his father."

"When did you find all this out?"

"While you were vacationing in the mountains."

"Some vacation." Jennie scooted next to him and rested her head on his shoulder.

"I know, princess. I'm sorry." He put an arm around her shoulders and hugged her close. "I shouldn't be joking about it."

"Dad?"

"Hmm."

"If Philippe shot this José guy, what happened to the gun?"

"Another good question and one I'm still puzzling over. He wouldn't have had time to take it off the premises. But we haven't been able to find any sign of it at the crime scene. And if he'd taken it with him, the EMTs or ER staff would have found it."

"Unless Philippe killed him earlier, got rid of the gun, then came back and started the fire."

"Thought of that too, princess." Dad yawned and stretched. "Let's not talk about it anymore tonight. I'm too tired to deal with it."

Jennie said good-night to Dad, then looked in on Nick and Carlos, said her prayers, and went to bed. After an hour of tossing and turning, she got up and crept downstairs to get some milk. She poured herself a glass and was taking it back to her room when a car pulled into the driveway. Lisa.

Jennie stepped out onto the porch and waited for her cousin to join her. "What are you doing out so late?"

"I was with Rafael, and we got to talking about that man who was killed."

Jennie dropped down onto the top step. "And . . ."

"We think we know who did it."

"Who?"

"Mr. Beaumont."

"How do you figure that?" Despite the fact that Jennie had listed his name on her suspect list, hearing Lisa say it out loud made the notion sound ridiculous. Still, in mysteries anyway, it was often the least likely person who turned out to be the bad guy.

"Think about it, Jen." Lisa sat on the second step and leaned against the railing. "Mr. Beaumont has been having financial trouble. He hired immigrants to work for him. Maybe he figured he could earn some extra money on the side by bringing in illegals and blackmailing them. Rafael thinks he might have hired José to work for him and was letting him stay in the church basement."

"That doesn't make any sense. Why would he use the church when he had a vacant warehouse?" Jennie drained her glass and set it down next to her.

"Maybe that's why it's empty. Maybe he thought he could make more money by firing all those people and using his warehouse as a storage facility."

Jennie wasn't certain why she felt she needed to defend Beaumont—maybe it was because of B.J. and Allison. They'd be devastated if their father turned out to be a killer. Besides, while some of what Lisa was saying seemed plausible, some didn't.

"Lisa, think a minute. If Mr. Beaumont was using his warehouse as a holding place for illegals until they could be given phony papers, why would he offer to let us use it as a school?"

"Greed." Lisa shot back the answer without hesitation. "Remember what Gavin said about Beaumont renting the building out? I went over there to help work on it yesterday. The school only takes up about half of the building. There's a full basement and a top floor. And there's something else. Rafael says the police don't even know this, but Beaumont opened a clothing manufacturing plant down in Mexico the first of the year under another name. Rafael thinks they're shipping up truckloads of clothing and probably have a partition or something where they can hide the illegals."

"That's very interesting, Lisa." The door behind them banged shut as Jason McGrady stepped outside.

"Uncle Jason!" Lisa jumped up. "You scared me!"

Dad didn't apologize. "Your mother's on the phone. You were supposed to call her when you got here."

"I forgot. It's okay if I spend the night, isn't it?"

"Sure, it'll probably take you that long to explain what this business with illegal immigrants is all about and why you think Beaumont is behind it."

"I was planning to tell you, Uncle J., but I wanted to run it by Jennie first."

Lisa and Jennie followed Dad inside, where Lisa repeated

nearly word for word what she had told Jennie earlier. Dad thanked her and said he'd take it from there. "Believe it or not, girls, the police can operate without your help. I'm sure we would have eventually found out about the plant in Mexico. I'll admit it does sound like a good lead. How did you find out?"

Lisa grinned. "Rafael said he knew about the factory because his mom and older sister used to work there but didn't know anything about bringing illegals in. When he heard about José he put two and two together."

Dad nodded. "I'll be sure to send him a thank-you note. Now, you two get to bed." He ran his hand through his thick dark hair. "Looks like another sleepless night."

By morning Lisa was feeling as terrible as Jennie about Mr. Beaumont being a suspect in the murder investigation. Dad was gone when they woke up, and the boys were still asleep.

"We need to go see Allison and B.J. They'll be devastated if it turns out their dad is guilty," Jennie said. "Maybe your mom will watch Nick and Carlos."

"You're right. But, please, Jennie, don't tell them I'm the one who told Uncle Jason. I hope they won't be mad at us."

"Well, I hope it doesn't turn out to be Mr. Beaumont."

Lisa sighed. "Who else would it be? He's the one with all the money and power. And he's kind of arrogant—like he thinks he's better than other people."

"I don't know about that. Mr. B. can act stuck-up sometimes, but he's a kind man. Look at what he did for Allison's boyfriend that time. And he hired a lawyer for Philippe and found jobs for Manuel and Philippe—" Jennie stopped. There was no point defending him. They'd find out the truth soon enough. Dad would have launched a full-scale investigation by now. It was out of their hands.

Rafael called at eight to thank Jennie and Lisa for their help. "The police arrive a few minutes ago," he said. "They have taken Mr. Beaumont in for questioning. Soon they will see that he is guilty and Philippe will be released."

"How are B.J. and Allison?" Jennie asked. "It must be terrible for them."

"It is a sad day for everyone."

Jennie sighed. "I suppose you want to talk to Lisa."

"Sí. If you would be so kind as to put her on."

Jennie handed the phone to Lisa and headed for the stairs to check on Nick and Carlos. It wasn't like Nick to sleep so late. Jennie was halfway up the stairs when the door to Nick's bedroom opened. He barreled right for her.

"Jennie! Jennie! He's gone. I woked up and I can't find him anyplace."

"Whoa. Slow down. Bernie's here. I just fed him."

"No, not Bernie," Nick wailed. "Carlos! Carlos is gone!"

22

After searching the rest of the house, Jennie carried Nick into the kitchen. "Carlos is gone," she told Lisa, who was still on the phone. "You'd better tell Rafael, then I'll need to call Dad. We've got to find him."

"Oh no." Lisa gave Rafael the information. "Okay, sounds like a good idea. Let us know if you find him." Handing the phone back to Jennie, she said, "Rafael's going to drive back this way—maybe Carlos is trying to get to the Beaumonts'."

Jennie nodded and dialed her father's number, letting him know what had happened.

"I'll get people on it right away. Stay put."

After hanging up, Jennie turned her attention back to Nick.

"Can we go look for him, Jennie?"

She hugged him close. "Not right now. Dad said we needed to stay here. The police will find him. Come on." She settled him on the chair. "How about some cereal and juice?"

"Is Carlos going to jail?"

"No, Nick." Jennie took a bowl and glass out of the cupboard and set them on the table.

"They don't put kids in jail for running away." Lisa pulled out the chair beside him.

"No, not for running away. For starting the fire."

Jennie nearly dropped the cereal. "Why would you say something like that? Did he tell you he started the fire?"

Nick shrank back. Covering his mouth, he shook his head. "No, no, no."

Jennie and Lisa exchanged glances. "Nick, this is very important. If Carlos told you something, you need to tell me."

"It's a secret. He made me promise."

"Come on, Nick. Remember what Mom said about secrets? There are good ones and bad ones. If it's a bad one, you need to tell."

"But I don't want him to get in trouble."

Jennie took a deep breath. "Okay, Nick. I'll guess and you tell me if I'm right, okay?"

"Okay."

"Carlos told you he started the fire."

Nick shook his head.

"Did he tell you who did?"

Nick shook his head again.

Before Jennie could question him more, the police arrived. Jennie gave them as much information as she could, and after making a search of the house and grounds, they spread out over the neighborhood, checking with neighbors and combing the area. When they'd gone she returned to the kitchen, where Lisa was still trying to coax an answer out of him.

"Come on, Nick. You can tell us. What did Carlos say?"

He put his hands over his mouth again.

Jennie carried him into the living room and sat him down on the sofa. "Let's try this again. Is Carlos afraid someone will hurt him?"

Nick's eyes grew larger. He nodded.

"Who? Did he tell you?"

"He can't tell 'cause his dad might have to stay in jail forever."

"His dad did it after all?" Jennie felt thoroughly confused.

The phone rang. Lisa ran into the kitchen to answer it. "Yes," Lisa said. Then after a few seconds, "No kidding. That's great. We'll be right there."

Jennie set Nick aside and joined Lisa in the kitchen. "Someone found him?"

"Rafael. Carlos is at the Beaumonts'."

Jennie heaved a deep sigh. "Let's get you dressed, little buddy. We're going to pick up Carlos. Now that he's talking, maybe we can find out who really did start that fire."

"If he even knows," Lisa said.

Jennie called her dad but didn't get an answer, then let dispatch know that Carlos had been found and was safe. Minutes later they were on their way to the Beaumonts'.

Even before she rang the bell, Jennie knew something was wrong. She attributed it at first to the fact that Mr. Beaumont had been taken in for questioning. Allison opened the door, her blue eyes fearful as though she were trying to tell them something. She didn't speak as she stepped back to let them in.

"What's that noise?" Jennie thought she heard someone moaning.

The door slammed behind them. Jennie spun around.

Lisa squealed. "What are you—?" Her mouth moved, but no sound came out.

Jennie pulled Nick close behind her. "It was you. All this time." Jennie wasn't surprised. Just disappointed. She'd read the darkness in his eyes but had never dreamed he'd turn out to be a killer.

"Move." Rafael waved the gun at them, herding them toward the basement stairs. "The others are waiting."

"Why—?" Lisa turned back to look at him.

Rafael had the decency to look penitent. "Oh, Lisa, I did not mean for this to happen. José and I, we bring many friends and families into United States. It is chance for a better life. But José take too much money. We argue and I—"

"You shot him and started the fire," Jennie finished.

"Carlos started the fire. I was going to put it out but saw that it would destroy the evidence, so I left it burning."

"You . . . you—" Lisa lashed out at him, knocking him off balance.

Seeing an opening, Jennie slammed into him. He slipped on the top stair and fell backward, firing a shot as he went down.

Jennie heard a swishing sound and felt something brush by her head. She'd been shot, but it didn't hurt much—just burned a little. Unable to catch herself, she fell forward, landing on her assailant.

Lisa screamed. Someone shouted to get down. Jennie heard voices, but they seemed to grow more and more distant. Then she heard nothing at all.

23

From the familiar scent of antiseptic and the sound of instruments dropping into metal bowls, Jennie knew where she was before she even opened her eyes. "She's coming to," someone said.

"I'm almost done. Couple more stitches."

Jennie's eyes drifted open.

A woman wearing bloody surgical gloves smiled down at her. "Hi. Glad you finally decided to join us."

"What happened?" Jennie vaguely remembered tackling Rafael and falling on top of him on the stairs.

"I think I'll let Lieutenant McGrady answer that." She glanced toward the curtain. "Tell him he can come in."

Moments later, Dad stood over the gurney, his hand gripping hers. "Princess. You and I are going to have to start coordinating things a little better."

"Huh?"

"Never mind." His dark gaze moved over her face and linked up with her own. "How are you feeling?"

"Okay. Did you get Rafael? He's the one who killed José and—"

"I know all about it. In fact, we were on our way to arrest him."

"How did you figure it out?"

"Talked to Jared again. He identified the people he saw

at the scene. Said when you and he were talking, he remembered a Hispanic guy coming out of the basement. I showed him Philippe's mug shot, thinking it was him, but it wasn't Philippe at all. Jared said he thought it might have been one of the kids he'd seen at the youth meeting he went to. We had our artist do a sketch from his description and guess who we came up with?"

"Rafael."

"I should have picked it up when you and I were talking last night. Rafael told you José had been shot in the head. He couldn't have known that unless he'd been there. We didn't release that information to the press until later that night."

"All done." The doctor rolled her chair back and pulled off her gloves. "We had to shave off a little of your hair, above your ear, but you have lots left to cover the bald spot. The wound will be uncomfortable for the next few days. Put ice on it and I'll write you a prescription for pain pills." She patted Jennie's arm and left the cubicle.

Jennie reached up and touched the square gauze dressing and the skin around it.

"It'll grow back, princess," Dad assured her. "The important thing is that you're still alive and that Rafael didn't get a chance to carry out his plan."

"What was he going to do?"

"He was running scared. He figured sooner or later Carlos would talk and that Beaumont would eventually put two and two together. I'm not sure how he did it, but he must have taken Carlos from our place sometime during the night. Lisa says her key to our house is missing, so he probably got in that way after I left and you girls went to bed."

"Poor Lisa. She must feel awful."

"She's more mad than sad, I think. Especially when she realized what he was up to."

"I can just about guess. He planned on putting us in the movie room and starting another fire. I thought I saw Mr.

Beaumont down there. Wasn't he supposed to be in jail?"

"We had him in for questioning and released him. Beaumont said when he came home he started asking Rafael about the situation. Rafael pulled a gun on him and took him back to the house. He had the entire family down there."

"And was waiting for us. I can't believe he'd kill that many people to cover his tracks."

"You know, Rafael isn't that much different than Rich when it comes down to it. Both men were willing to kill to further their cause. They were both prejudiced. Now they are both going to face life imprisonment."

"How is Carlos?"

"He's fine now that he's back with his dad. Told us everything. He had been playing with matches and set a fire in a wastebasket. He'd heard the shot and saw Rafael coming out of the room near the furnace. Rafael set the wastebasket in the room and pulled Carlos out. Told Philippe Carlos had started the fire and they'd need to get out. Rafael told Carlos he'd better keep his mouth shut if he ever expected to see his dad again."

"Poor little guy. No wonder he was so frightened." Jennie yawned. It had been a bizarre case, but thank God it was over. Almost over.

"What about Reverend Cole? What's going to happen to her?"

"She's been released. She'll be seeing a therapist for a while, but she seemed in pretty good spirits. I think she'll do just fine."

Two days later, Jennie stood on a hill in Mount Tabor Cemetery with her parents and Nick, Lisa, Aunt Kate, Uncle Kevin, Kurt, the Beaumonts, Gavin Winslow and his parents, Reverend Cole, and Michael's sister, Ashley, along with all the kids from the youth group and dozens of other members of the Trinity congregation. Jared was there as well, flanked by two men, federal agents for protection, Jennie guessed.

They'd all come to pay their last respects to a man they all had come to love. Pastor Dave gave the eulogy, saying how Michael would have been proud of the way they'd come together and that his dream to make Trinity a home to everyone, regardless of race or culture, was becoming a reality.

"As we say good-bye to our brother, let's keep our hearts and minds attuned to the way Michael lived. Let us love God with all of our hearts and minds and souls, and let us love one another as Christ first loved us."

Jennie's watery gaze fell to the rose she held in her hand. Taking her turn, she walked forward and dropped her rose on the casket. "Good-bye, Michael. I'll miss you."

"I'll miss you, too, Jennie," she could almost hear him say.

Dad wrapped an arm around her shoulder and whispered, "He was one of the good guys."

"Yes, he was," Mom said as she, too, dropped her rose. "We'll all miss him."

"Mama?" interjected Nick. "If Michael is in heaven, why are we putting his flowers in the ground?"

Several people nearby chuckled.

Jennie stifled a smile.

"That's a very good question." Mom knelt down beside him. "Would you like to put your flower somewhere else?"

He nodded. "Up in the tree, then Michael can reach down and get it."

Dad lifted him up while he deposited his flower.

Jennie would have given anything if Michael had survived the fire. But as Ashley had reminded all of them, in heaven Michael would experience complete healing and was in a far better place. Jennie was glad about one thing. She'd had the opportunity to capture the man responsible for the fire. In this case, at least, justice would be served.

"Jennie?" Dad's soft mellow voice broke into her thoughts. "Are you ready? We need to get your mother home."

"Sure. Let me say hi to Jared first."

"Don't be long."

"I won't."

"Hi," Jennie said as she approached him. "Um . . . just want to see how you're holding up."

"Okay. I'm staying with a foster family right now. They're nice."

An awkward silence stretched between them as they stood on the hillside looking down at the grave.

"Well," Jennie said finally. "I should go. Mom's going to have a baby, and she tires out pretty easily."

"That's neat. I—I'm glad we got a chance to talk. I want to tell you how sorry I am about Rich abducting you. If I hadn't lied to him about being in jail he wouldn't have—"

Jennie stopped him. "Don't worry about it. I don't blame you. Besides, it came out okay. We're both safe and you're free to live the kind of life you want."

"I'm not sure, but I think I know what that's going to be." He glanced toward the grave. "I'd like to pattern my life after Michael's. When the trial is over, I'll go to college and maybe seminary. First though"—he gave her a lopsided grin—"I need to let my hair grow out."

"Oh," she teased. "I was just getting used to it." After another long pause she said, "I'd better go."

"Yeah, me too." He reached forward and gave her a hug. "Thanks for believing in me."

Jennie smiled. "Thank Michael—and God."

On the way home, Jennie leaned back against the seat and

closed her eyes. Her brushes with death, both with Rich and Rafael, might have deterred some, but Jennie McGrady was more determined than ever to become a lawyer. She just hoped the next case would be a while in coming.

Teen Series From Bethany House Publishers

Early Teen Fiction (11–14)

HIGH HURDLES by Lauraine Snelling
Show jumper DJ Randall strives to defy the odds and achieve her dream of winning Olympic Gold.

SUMMERHILL SECRETS by Beverly Lewis
Fun-loving Merry Hanson encounters mystery and excitement in Pennsylvania's Amish country.

THE TIME NAVIGATORS by Gilbert Morris
Travel back in time with Danny and Dixie as they explore unforgettable moments in history.

Young Adult Fiction (12 and up)

CEDAR RIVER DAYDREAMS by Judy Baer
Experience the challenges and excitement of high school life with Lexi Leighton and her friends—over one million books sold!

GOLDEN FILLY SERIES by Lauraine Snelling
Readers are in for an exhilarating ride as Tricia Evanston races to become the first female jockey to win the sought-after Triple Crown.

JENNIE MCGRADY MYSTERIES by Patricia Rushford
A contemporary Nancy Drew, Jennie McGrady's sleuthing talents promise to keep readers on the edge of their seats.

LIVE! FROM BRENTWOOD HIGH by Judy Baer
When eight teenagers invade the newsroom, the result is an action-packed teen-run news show exploring the love, laughter, and tears of high school life.

THE SPECTRUM CHRONICLES by Thomas Locke
Adventure and romance await readers in this fantasy series set in another place and time.

SPRINGSONG BOOKS by various authors
Compelling love stories and contemporary themes promise to capture the hearts of readers.

WHITE DOVE ROMANCES by Yvonne Lehman
Romance, suspense, and fast-paced action for teens committed to finding pure love.

9608